RETURN TO LOVE

Holly felt she needed a break and, with her young son, Michael, went to stay with her Aunt Jo in Felswithen, Yorkshire. Holly had been brought up there, but had not been back for five years. She was shocked to discover that Eden Pemberley, her former lover, had returned to the village. It had taken her a long time to forget Eden, and now he was back in her life again. But Holly knew she must not tell him he was the father of her child.

MARY MACKIE

RETURN TO LOVE

Complete and Unabridged

LINFORD
Leicester

First published in Great Britain in 1979

First Linford Edition
published 1997

British Library CIP Data

Mackie, Mary
    Return to love.—Large print ed.—
    Linford romance library
    1. Love stories
    2. Large type books
    I. Title
    823.9'14 [F]

    ISBN 0–7089–5116–3

Published by
F. A. Thorpe (Publishing) Ltd.
Anstey, Leicestershire

Set by Words & Graphics Ltd.
Anstey, Leicestershire
Printed and bound in Great Britain by
T. J. International Ltd., Padstow, Cornwall

This book is printed on acid-free paper

1

IT was a peaceful view. Beyond the field gate where Holly leaned, farmland stretched out across rolling hills. The sun was going down in a glory of golden clouds, but the breeze was cool. She pulled her jacket more firmly round her and one pale, slender hand smoothed back a blowing tendril of apricot hair.

Her eyes were not on the view but turned inwards on to another landscape — a wild, lonely place where heather stretched purple across the moor. Tomorrow she thought, I shall be back there, and a shiver ran through her, half joyful anticipation and half fear. What would she find at Felswithen? Was it a mistake to return?

Abruptly she became aware that the man beside her had spoken and was

1

now regarding her with a glimmer of irritation in his hazel eyes.

"I'm sorry, Peter," she apologised softly. "What did you say?"

He placed firm hands on her shoulders, almost shaking her. "Where are you this evening, Holly? You've been in a dream ever since we came out. Have you forgotten this is the last time we shall see each other for a while?"

"No, of course I haven't forgotten," Holly replied. She regretted having offended him, but Felswithen called to her, making Sussex seem unreal. Even after five years, the spell was still potent.

"I don't think you ought to go," Peter said abruptly, turning away to lean on the gate, the sun gilding his sandy hair. "I have a feeling something awful will happen to you."

"That's nonsense," Holly gently chided him. "I need this break. I need to think about the future. Before grandfather died, things were different, but uncle William and his new wife have made it clear they don't want me at the farm much longer. I must think again. I have a son to support, you know."

"I know." He whirled suddenly to face her, fierce emotions burning in his eyes. "Marry me, Holly. I'll take care of you and Michael. I'll treat him as if he were my own son. Don't go to Yorkshire."

There was no joy on Holly's face, only amazement and uncertainty. This was one complication she had hoped to avoid, just another problem to add to the growing list.

"Isn't it the ideal answer?" Peter asked. "I can support you. I'll buy a house. Michael needs a father. You've bravely tried to bring him up alone and I admire you for it, but . . . For Michael's sake, marry me!"

It was emotional blackmail, Holly thought, to appeal to her through her son. Peter was a good man and he would be kind to Michael, who already liked him. But was that reason enough for marriage? She had always believed there should be something more between a man and a woman, some spark that could not be denied. Was that just wishful thinking?

Part of these thoughts must have shown in her eyes, for Peter sighed. "You don't have to answer me now. Think about it while you're away, if you must go."

"I must," she replied, kneading her achinghead with her fingers. "I need to get right away and think about everything. But thank you, Peter."

The frown on his face slowly turned to understanding and deep concern. She did need a holiday. She was so thin he could have spanned her waist with his two hands, and beneath her green eyes there were violet shadows.

"Let me take you home," he said gently. "You need a good night's sleep before you tackle that long journey."

The following morning, Holly and Michael embarked on the train which would take them north. Mid-afternoon found them aboard a coach being

4

pulled by a brightly-painted steam engine, though the view was obscured through condensation on the windows. It had been raining hard for most of the day.

Closing her eyes, she tried to picture Peter Hastings' face, but it too was lost in a mist. Other memories came insistently, memories of the last summer she had spent at Beck Lodge.

It was strange how she could still picture Eden Pemberley as clearly as if she had just seen him. Eden, with his dark hair and black, clever eyes that could change mood in the space of a split second. Holly had first seen him on the moors, riding a mettlesome black stallion which kept shifting beneath him as he spoke to Holly, asking her name and warning her of the hidden mine shafts. Broad shoulders strained the material of a cream shirt that was open at the neck to display his tanned throat, and denim jeans and shining boots encased his long legs.

No! Opening her eyes, Holly willed

the picture away. Eden was far from here, living in the United States, in California, so the newspapers said. Had he not been, she would never have dared to come back.

For five years she had followed Eden's career and personal life through the gossip columns. Newspapers reported each new exhibition of his paintings, his romances and eventual marriage to the lovely starlet Lucy Bennett. Then had come rumours of a divorce and the shocking end to the marriage when Lucy had drowned after a party on a yacht. There had even been speculation that Eden might have been implicated, but the girl's death was eventually declared an accident, though it left a nasty question-mark over Eden's reputation.

For herself, Holly did not know what to think. The Eden of the jet-set was not the Eden she had come to know five years before — or, more correctly, the Eden she thought she had known. It was clear to her now that the man who had captivated her that sun-drenched summer was mostly a delusion, a fairy-tale prince dreamed up out of her own imagination and her longing for love.

The train hooted three times, warning of its imminent arrival in the small station. Holly woke Michael and, when the train stopped, lifted him down to the platform to stand beside the heavy case and holdall. From beneath the brim of a scarlet rain hat, his dark eyes were alight with excitement, reminding Holly sharply of Eden.

"Holly! Hello!" Without warning, here was Aunt Jo, bearing down on them with a wide smile and a huge black umbrella. Somehow she managed to embrace Holly and then sweep Michael up all in one wide movement before leading the way to the mud-spattered land-rover beyond the station gate.

Josephine Dailie was a tall, angular woman in her late forties, dressed now in a voluminous raincoat which met the tops of sturdy boots. A woollen hat was pulled unceremoniously over her short grey hair.

"What a day!" She sighed. "More like autumn than summer. In you go, Michael, that's a good boy."

Travelling through a tree-cloaked valley, the vehicle emerged into open countryside, climbing steadily towards the hills ahead. Green fields stretched upwards to where low cloud hid the hill-tops. It was lonely country, the houses in small huddles, built of the same grey stone as the network of walls which lay across the slopes.

They turned into a smaller dale, where the road was uneven and narrow. At the far end of the dale, Beck Lodge sat squarely on the hillside, its low slate roof blending with the mass of the hill behind it, outlines softened by the branches of one single great larch tree which grew behind the house. The windows of the lodge were small, set in thick walls, and beyond the front porch one stepped straight into the main room, where a welcoming fire was blazing.

Holly caught her breath. The rest of the room seemed to grow indistinct as she stared at that portrait of a girl seated among purple heather. Long hair like pail copper floated across her shoulders and on her face was a look of dreamy enchantment as she looked down at the sprig of heather she was holding, which the artist had etched delicately against the folds of a white full skirt.

"It's a copy," Jo Dailie said. "He wouldn't sell me the original. It went on exhibition in London, you know."

"Did it?" Holly was annoyed that her voice should be choked. She cleared her throat and made an effort at lightness. "No, how on earth would I know? Aunt Jo, I . . . I'd like to have a wash and unpack, if I may."

"Of course. You go ahead. I'll look after Michael."

The bedroom window, under sloping eaves, looked out on the hill which towered behind the house. The branches of the larch were tossing in the wind and darkness was coming early because of the heavy cloud. Rain trickled down the window like slow tears.

Holly swallowed the sickness in her throat, trying to beat back the wave of memory which threatened to overwhelm her. How could her aunt have bought that picture? But aunt Jo didn't know what it would mean to Holly. Only Holly knew, and Eden. Eden . . .

They had met only twice before he asked if he could paint her. She had been flattered, and pleased because it meant being more in his company. She had been eighteen, sheltered by a lifetime in her grandfather's care. Nothing had prepared her for the onslaught to her emotions which Eden Pemberley had performed so effortlessly. Holly had been enchanted, by the moors and by the man.

She turned abruptly from the window. No, not enchanted, she amended the thought bitterly. Taken for a fool was more like it. She had been an innocent seduced by a scoundrel, though her memory told her there had been tenderness, too. Angrily she rebuked the idea. Eden had shown not the slightest interest after she left Felswithen. Instead he had gone back to his former life-style and eventual marriage to Lucy Bennett. And she, Holly, had been left with Michael as a constant reminder of one reckless moment — the only one in her life — when everything she had been taught had been blown into non-existence by the kisses of a cheat.

She had always sworn she would never come back to Felswithen. No one must ever suspect the true identity of Michael's father, which she had guarded fiercely, out of pride and out of fear. Pride because Eden had not tried to find her, had not even written; and fear because, if he did find out about the child, Eden would think she had done it to trap him. The

Pemberleys had everything, while Holly had nothing. Except that now she had Michael.

When she had unpacked, she washed and changed into denims and a loose sweater before going down to find Michael being given his tea in the cosy kitchen.

"Was he hungry?" she asked.

"I should just think he was!" her aunt exclaimed. "You've been travelling all day. I made a casserole for us," she added with a nod at the Aga cooker, "but Michael couldn't wait. Anyway, it's just about bedtime, isn't it, young man?"

Michael claimed that he wasn't tired, but made few complaints when Holly took him upstairs to the smallest bedroom and put him to bed.

"Is he asleep?" her aunt asked, beginning to serve a thick brown casserole which smelt delicious.

"Went out like a light, bless him. I did wonder how he would react to being in a strange place. This is the first

12

time he's slept away from the farm."

Jo's eyes were appraising as they rested on Holly's face. "A change will do him good. And you too, my dear."

"I won't deny I'm in need of a break," Holly admitted ruefully.

"You could have come before. I've asked you often enough. I offered to fetch you and . . . " Bitting her lip, the older woman sighed. "But there's little enough to do here, I know. I expect you've been busy with your own life."

"Yes." She could hardly tell her aunt the real reason for her reluctance to come back to Yorkshire.

"And what do you intend to do now? Your uncle William won't need you to keep house for him now he's married, I suppose. I can't help thinking it would have been an awful lot easier if you had had Michael adopted. You gave up an awful lot for that child — your teacher-training, your marriage prospects . . . "

A cold finger seemed to touch Holly's heart. "I gave it up because I chose to.

He's someone of my very own, Aunt Jo. That's something I've never had before. I don't even remember my parents. All my life I've been an interloper in someone else's house. Michael has given me a purpose."

"He has also given you a good many problems," Jo replied. "But I know how it must have been — you felt like Cinderella and when the prince came riding by you thought it was for keeps."

Now Holly felt her face grow hot, with shame and with anger. Bright spots of colour on her cheeks gave her eyes an added brightness. "What do you mean?"

"Why . . . " Jo said in amazement. "Only that you were too young to know the difference. You needed someone and he came along, whoever he was."

Holly wished she had bitten her tongue instead of letting the words burst out, but that remark about a prince riding had been too near the truth. He had come riding, literally, on a stallion as black as coal. But he had not carried her off to live happily ever after. No, it had been no fairy tale and Eden Pemberley was no chivalrous prince.

"You know who he was," she said repeating the lie she had told so often. "He was a student who came to help with the harvest. I'm sorry, Aunt Jo, but everyone keeps telling me what a fool I was to keep Michael. I don't regret it, not for a moment. He's my son and I love him. I'll do anything in my power to see that he has a happy, normal life."

"I know you will, my dear," Jo said. "I'm only thinking of you. Shall we take our coffee into the sitting room?"

She found herself telling her aunt about Peter Hastings and his sudden proposal just the evening before. It made the hurtful memories retreat into a corner of her mind as she spoke of Peter's kindness. He had been a good friend to her. It seemed to Holly that she had two choices: she could marry

Peter, or she could try to find a home for herself and Michael, and a job to pay for it.

"You're too proud, that's your trouble," Jo commented. "I suppose you think Peter is sorry for you. He sounds as though he would made a good husband."

"Oh, he would," Holly replied at once, "but . . . I don't love him, Aunt Jo. How can I marry a man I don't respond to?"

"If you're talking about physical attraction, there's a lot more to marriage than that," Jo told her briskly. "Don't confuse a stable relationship with something like you felt for Eden Pemberley."

Startled, Holly flicked a questioning glance at her aunt.

"Well, really, my dear," Jo said with a laugh. "You were transparent that summer. You had the most awful crush on Eden, didn't you? I expect you realise now that he was not your type, apart from being much too old

16

for you. Why, he must have been nearly thirty even then, and you just out of school. You've probably read about the scandals he's been involved in since then."

It was a relief to Holly that her aunt had misread the situation. For one awful moment she had thought that Jo had guessed the truth.

"It was just a pity that you had to go home suffering from the effects of that infatuation," Jo went on. "I'm sure that's what made you so vulnerable to that young man who was working at the farm. Holly, dear . . . don't take this amiss, but up here people tend to . . . I mean the permissive age hasn't really reached this far and I've . . . I've told my friends that you're a widow."

"Oh," Holly said flatly.

"Yes, dear. I thought it was best — for you, I mean. Goodness knows I understand absolutely, but other people . . . you do see my point?"

"Of course," Holly said quietly. It saddened her to realise that Jo had been shocked by Michael's arrival, whatever she might say to the contrary. She wanted to explain that it hadn't been a casual thing, it had meant something, at the time, that she had loved Eden dearly and believed he loved her, and it happened once, just the once! But she couldn't afford to excuse herself, so she added, "There's just one problem, Aunt Jo — I don't have a wedding ring. I would have, if I were a widow, wouldn't I?"

"Oh, yes. I thought of that." Jo's relief was evident as she stood up, a lanky figure in loose-fitting twill trousers and a hand-knitted pullover, and took down from the mantelpiece a small box which she handed to Holly. "It's only a cheap one. It may not fit very closely, but no one's going to notice. It's just for the sake of appearances."

Holly looked with distaste at the thin gold hand in the velvet-lined box and she was once again aware of the dreamy smile on the face of the girl in

18

the portrait. Because of that portrait, because of her silly dreams, she had had to tell lies, and now she must act a lie or shame Aunt Jo.

With a bitter twist to her lips, she slipped the ring on her finger. It was a little loose, but it would serve its purpose.

At that moment there was a terrible cracking sound that seemed to fill the valley. Holly leaped to her feet, staring wide-eyed at her aunt.

"What . . . " The words were drowned by a deafening crash and a clatter of falling bricks. The house trembled. There was the faint tinkle of shattered glass, then the lights went out and an awful silence closed about the house.

"Aunt Jo . . . " Holly breathed into the firelit gloom.

"Wait!" the answer came crisply. "I've got a torch somewhere. Just stay where you are, Holly."

Holly obeyed, waiting dry-mouthed until her aunt re-emerged from the kitchen with a heavy-duty torch whose beam was like a search-light. Cautiously, Jo ventured outside by the front door.

Fear and uncertainty immobilised Holly. She heard a vague sound in the distance which eventually identified itself as an engine, coming at speed along the dale road. It slowed as it approached and the driver must have noticed that something was wrong for the car stopped and Holly, watching from the window, saw a man climb out to be met by her aunt. Together the two went out of sight round the corner of the house.

What on earth had happened? Holly wondered. Then the torchlight reappeared and her aunt returned to the house, the man a dark shadow behind her.

"It's the tree," Jo said in a strained voice. "It's come down right across the back corner of the house. The roof's all smashed, and a great chunk of the wall The tree's just leaning there."

As she came further into the room the man behind her stepped forward, so that the firelight licked over him. He stared at Holly, then glanced at the portrait above the hearth as if to make sure of her identity.

Holly could hardly breathe. The man who appeared so suddenly out of the night was the man she had thought was half the world away; the man whom only in her worst nightmares had she dreamed of meeting again — Eden Pemberley.

"Holly's just arrived for a holiday," her aunt said. "Excuse me, I must have a look at the back bedroom."

She left them alone, facing each other across the flickering sitting room. Holly saw his lips twist derisively, the black eyes catching the glow of the flames, seeming demonic in his grim face.

And then she heard Michael crying. Stumbling from the room, she fled up the night-black stairs.

2

WRAPPING Michael in a blanket, Holly lifted him in her arms and he stopped crying, holding her tightly round her neck. She heard her aunt return downstairs, her voice mingling with Eden Pemberley's dark brown tones. Poor Aunt Jo. It was terrible.

Trembling, Holly realised that Eden's presence was equally terrible. He was here, and his son was here. She held Michael's head to her cheek, the soft curls caressing her lips, and her arms were hard and protective. Coming back to Felswithen had been an insane thing to do.

A vagrant gleam of fitful moonlight caught on the slim gold band she was wearing on her wedding finger, and suddenly the ring seemed like a talisman, protecting against evil. She would say she had been married. Eden need never know it was a lie. It would stop him from wondering.

The thoughts rushed round her head crazily, panic and terror and fierce maternal love mixed with anxiety for her aunt. What would Jo do now? Suppose the house were unsafe?

Torchlight beamed along the hall and came through the door, briefly blinding Holly as it fell across her face.

"Sorry," her aunt's voice said from behind the light. "How's Michael? Was he frightened?"

"A little, but it was only the noise. He's fine now. Aunt Jo . . . how bad is it?"

"Pretty bad." The tone was brave but her despair and weariness came through. "There's a branch of the tree inside your bedroom, bricks and plaster everywhere. The electricity cable is down, so there's no power, and your bed is wet through. One thing's for sure, Holly — you and Michael can't

23

stay here. If you'll pack your things, Mr Pemberley has offered to take you up to Hawks High for a few nights, until I see what has to be done."

A chill had settled over Holly. "Hawks High? But Aunt Jo . . . I can't!"

"Then where do you suggest?" Jo said tartly, but checked herself. "I'm sorry. I don't much care for the idea, either, but we must put Michael first. He'll be much safer up at Hawks High for a while. Sir Matthew won't mind, I'm sure. And to be honest I shall have enough on my plate without worrying about you two."

There was such desolation in her voice that Holly swallowed the arguments which had been on her lips. The thought of being at Hawks High made her stomach churn, but there was nothing she could do about it without making a ridiculous scene.

"All right, Aunt Jo," she said quietly, fetching the holdall to pack Michael's belongings.

Jo closed the door, saying in a taut undertone, "I'm afraid I may have said the wrong thing to Mr Pemberley. He asked what your married name was and in the heat of the moment I said 'Hastings'. It was the first name I could think of. So remember, you're Mrs Hastings."

Poor Peter, Holly thought as she repacked her own case in the ruined bedroom where rainwater, plaster and bricks made a messy mixture. He would not be any too pleased at having his name used for such a purpose.

Eden took the cases out to the car. He had not spoken a word to Holly, for which she was thankful. Then with a return of panic, she realised that Jo had not packed a bag for herself.

"Aren't you coming?" she gasped.

"What, and leave the house like this?" Jo retorted. "Certainly not! I can manage quite well on my own. I'll see you tomorrow some time."

Her throat constricted by nerves, her arms tightly round her son, Holly stepped out into the damp night. Clouds passed swiftly across the moon and the dale was filled with a rushing of wind. Eden stood holding the rear door of his car open, his black hair ruffled by the wind and his face shadowed.

Fighting a desire to flee, Holly set Michael on the back seat of the car and herself climbed after him.

As they drove across the shadowed valley, through the silver and black of the moonlight, Michael asked questions which she answered in a comforting tone. The man at the wheel said nothing. He might have been a taxi-driver for all the interest he showed.

Across the valley, the road turned once more towards the hills, gently climbing to a dark cleft between two crags. Where the ground opened out again, the misty moonlight played across a wide natural amphitheatre where Hawks High stood, grim and alone, its tall chimneys reaching up to the cloud-tossed sky.

Without a word, Eden climbed out

of the car and strode round to open the door for Holly, but by the time she had lifted Michael out, carrying him clear of the wet grass, Eden was on his way to the front door, where he deposited their luggage on the verandah.

"You'd better knock," he instructed Holly as he turned back to the car.

Bemused, she lifted the heavy knocker and brought it down sharply three times, awaking an echo in the surrounding hills. The car boot slammed down and Eden returned to the verandah carrying two large suitcases. He gave Holly one brief, unfriendly glance, and himself reached for the knocker.

Before the echoes died, the door came open and light shafted out to illuminate the three for the benefit of the round-shouldered, grey-haired man who stood there.

"Mr Eden!" he said with pleasure, opening the door wider to allow them inside.

The hall was wide, floored with red tiles on which rugs were scattered.

The stairs stretched up into blackness between dark oak-panelled walls hung with stags' heads and heavy-framed paintings.

"Where's my uncle?" Eden was asking.

"In the study, sir," the manservant replied. "I'm afraid there's no heat on in the sitting room. We weren't expecting you."

"No, I realise that. All right, Grimson, I'll announce myself."

Grimson glanced at Holly, his eyes sweeping over her speculatively before he turned away.

"This way, Mrs Hastings," Eden said tersely, leading the way down a passage to the right of the hall.

He entered the study without ceremony, ushering her after him. It was warm in there, a fire burning, wall lights lending a softness to the leather furniture and shelves groaning under the weight of hundreds of books. In a big armchair by the fire, Sir Matthew Pemberley had been reading, but he looked up in surprise at the disturbance.

Swiftly, Eden explained the problem, how the tree had fallen on Beck Lodge and he had thought it his duty to offer the shelter of Hawks High to Mrs Dailie's niece and her son.

"But of course, you did the right thing!" Sir Matthew exclaimed, beaming now at Holly. He stood up, light gleaming from his bald head and a quilted smoking-jacket belted round his ample waist. When he came to lead her to his own vacated chair, she realised he was scarcely as tall as she was.

"Sit down, my dear. You look frozen. And this young man ought to be in bed." With a smile, he chucked Michael under the chin. "Eden, ring for Mrs Grimson, will you? You should have brought Mrs Dailie along, too."

"I tried," Eden replied, shrugging off his overcoat to reveal dark brown shirt and slacks, "but she's a very stubborn lady."

They talked about Jo and the problems of clearing the tree, Sir

Matthew's pink pate tilted back as he addressed his tall nephew. The contrast between them was almost comical, though at that moment Holly was too tense to appreciate the humour of it.

Watching Eden, Holly was again aware of the powerful physical attraction of the man.

When Mrs Grimson arrived she proved to be a trim woman with brown hair drawn into a chignon. She looked too young to be the wife of the ageing manservant.

"I always keep one of the guest suites ready," she said when Sir Matthew had explained the situation. "Grimson has already taken their luggage up. Will Mr Eden be sleeping in the studio, as usual?"

"Naturally," Eden said, a dry note in his voice, "but I can make up the bed myself if I'm creating problems, Mrs Grimson."

"It's no problem," the housekeeper replied crisply. "If the young lady would like to come with me, I'll show her to her room."

"What a way to start a holiday!" Sir Matthew remarked to Holly with a smile. "But you're welcome, very welcome. Both of you."

Nervously uttering her thanks, Holly carried Michael in the wake of the housekeeper, managing to avoid Eden's eyes, for every time he glanced at her there was derision in his face, as if he scornfully remembered her naivety of five years previously. She was now sure that he regarded her as just one more conquest on a lengthy list.

"It must have been a terrible shock for your aunt," Mrs Grimson said as they climbed the broad stairway.

"Yes, it was, but she soon rallied. She's already planning how to start clearing up. But it was lucky that E . . . that Mr Pemberley was coming by."

"Him!" There was disapproval in the housekeeper's pleasant voice. "He turns up any time he pleases. Takes advantage of his uncle's kindness, if you want my opinion. I know he's the heir and one day he'll be master here, but all the same . . . Still, it's not my place to complain."

Along the upper hallway, Mrs Grimson showed Holly into a room decorated in blue and white. The furniture was gleaming mahogany, contrasting with the pale colours of walls, carpet and bedspread.

"The bathroom's here," Mrs Grimson said, throwing open a door to the left before crossing the room to another door. "And this is the little boy's room. You'll be nice and private in this suite."

Michael's room was a small version of Holly's, this time with a single bed and the battered holdall looking horribly shabby in a plump armchair. Holly set her son down on the floor, easing her aching arms.

"He does look tired, poor lamb," Mrs Grimson said tenderly. "Shall I bring him a glass of warm milk? And what about you, Mrs Hastings, will you be going down?"

Holly baulked at the thought, keeping her face averted as she bent to undo Michael's raincoat. "I think not. I'm very tired. Perhaps . . . is it possible for me to have a cup of coffee, please?"

"Of course. I'll bring the drinks at once."

Left alone with Michael, Holly undressed him for the second time that day. He had been very good but now he was yawning and growing fretful.

"It has been a funny old day, hasn't it?" Holly said gently. "Never mind, darling, you can go to sleep now. This is a lovely soft bed."

She sat him up with the pillows behind him. Suddenly her spirits had drooped and she wanted to weep in despair. She had nothing to give Michael except her love, but Eden, his father, had everything. It was intolerable that they should all be under one roof.

Sensing her mood, Michael was scowling fiercely, bringing a stab of pain to Holly's heart. How like Eden the child was! Having been with Eden again so recently, she could now see the startling similarity and a new terror assailed her. Suppose someone else noticed?

A brief knock at the door heralded the return of the housekeeper, whose sharp eyes went at once to Holly's face. "Are you all right, Mrs Hastings? Is something wrong?"

"No, nothing at all," Holly lied.

"Well, here's his milk and this is your coffee. Oh, look at the little cherub! Doesn't he look sweet? I envy you, Mrs Hastings. Grimson and I have no children."

She stood watching as Holly sat on Michael's bed, helping him drink the milk.

"Have you worked here long?" Holly asked.

She could have done without the long history which followed. Mrs Grimson,

34

it seemed, had worked for Sir Matthew and his late wife for years. She had known his son, who died of pneumonia when he was only nine years old, which was why Sir Matthew now took such an interest in Eden, according to Mrs Grimson. It was clear, however, that the housekeeper did not share her employer's opinion of his nephew.

"Grimson won't hear a word against Mr Eden," she said, "but what will happen when Sir Matthew goes I don't know. I might not like working for Mr Eden especially after . . . well, you probably saw it in the papers. His wife was drowned, you know."

"Yes, it was tragic," Holly put in.

Mrs Grimson glanced down at Michael, who was settling down to sleep, and added in an undertone, "They can say what they like, but those two never did get on. The rows! I've never heard anything like it in my life. I've seen him look at her as if for two pins he'd throttle her, so it wouldn't surprise me if he did tip her off that yacht. He knew she couldn't swim. Still, I mustn't keep you talking all night. Breakfast is at half past eight, in the dining room. Goodnight, Mrs Hastings. I hope you'll be comfortable."

Wishing that Mrs Grimson had kept her thoughts to herself, Holly took a hot bath and slipped between sheets of the finest linen. The circle of light from the bedside lamp was like a moon against the shadowed ceiling and outside the wind lashed across the moor, eddying wildly round the house in the hollow.

Despite the tumult in her mind, sleep came suddenly, bringing a welcome relief from thought. She was exhausted, mentally and physically, sleeping so deeply that no trace of dreams remained in the morning.

She became aware of Micahel chattering to himself close by. The chink of metal on metal roused her further and she opened her eyes to see her son sprawled full length on the floor driving a couple of toy cars round the pattern in the blue carpet. Bright sunlight beat against the curtains and beyond them the world was still. The wind dropped.

Shaking away the last dregs of sleep, Holly stretched and tossed her head so that her hair fell loosely round her shoulders.

"Look out!" Michael cried, deep in his game, as he brought the two cars into headlong collision. "Crash! Send for the ambulance!"

Smiling to herself, Holly threw back the covers and went barefoot to greet her son with a kiss. He seemed unaffected by the traumas of the previous day.

It was very warm, though it was barely eight o'clock. The weather must have remembered it was supposed to be summertime, Holly thought as she drew back the long drapes and threw the window wide open.

There was the hollow, the hills rising up to protect the old house. Their slopes were thick with curling bracken which gave way to heather near the summits. Above, the sky was a cloudless blue, as though the previous night's wind had scoured it clean, while below, at the bottom of the basin where the house stood, rough grass grew over the uneven ground, neatly nibbled by sheep. Three of the grey-woolled animals were peacefully cropping off to Holly's right, near the sleek, black Jaguar which had brought her to Hawks High.

A movement below drew her eyes to where Eden Pemberley had suddenly emerged from directly beneath her. Before she could move he had glanced up, his gaze licking arrogantly over her.

"Fine morning," he said pleasantly enough.

"Yes," Holly got out through the constriction in her throat, colour flaming in her pale cheeks.

"I'm going to Beck Lodge, to see what I can do for your aunt," he informed her. "Any messages?"

"No, thank you. Oh — yes, tell her

I'll be over to see her later."

His eyes narrowed, one corner of his mouth lifting wryly. "Anxious to get away, are you, Holly? Or should I say Mrs Hastings?"

The way he drawled the name made Holly take a sharp breath. Did he suspect that it wasn't really her name? But Eden had turned away, striding with that easy, pantherish grace which was deceptively lazy.

He couldn't know, she told herself firmly. It had simply been his way of mocking her.

In an act of deliberate self-abasement, she again put on her faded denims, though on that hot morning she accompanied them with a shirt-blouse that had been tie-dyed so that it was streaked with blue. Her hair she did in a thick plait to fall over one shoulder. She might as well look what she was — the no-account niece of a neighbour, here on sufferance. There was bitter defiance in her as she brushed Michael's shining curls, aware that his cotton shorts and

T-shirt were from a chain store, the cheapest she could find because she had to be very careful with money.

As they went hand in hand down the stairs, Mrs Grimson appeared in the gloomy hallway, exclaiming afresh over Michael. Holly did not argue when the housekeeper suggested that the little boy should eat in the kitchen, where he would be more comfortable, and Michael himself seemed happy enough with the arrangement. He went off chatting easily to the housekeeper in his usual friendly fashion.

The dining room opened from the hall. At the head of the long, polished table Sir Matthew was already seated.

"Good morning, my dear. I hope you slept well," he greeted her with a smile. "Help yourself to what you want. I'm afraid my nephew has already eaten. He was anxious to see if your aunt needed any assistance."

"That was very kind of him," Holly muttered, lifting the silver lid of one of the dishes on the sideboard. There were devilled kidneys beneath it, but her stomach revolted at the thought of food and she settled for a piece of toast.

"You're as bad as Eden," Sir Matthew said, looking askance at her plate as she took a seat. "When I said he had eaten it was an exaggeration. He breakfasted on coffee and nothing else, though he hardly touched his supper last night. Jet-lag, he said. Help yourself to coffee, my dear."

"Thank you." Holly lifted the heavy pot and the liquid steamed out, black and appetising. "Forgive my asking, Sir Matthew, but has E . . . your nephew recently arrived in the country?"

"Flew in yesterday, from California, you know. It appears he became suddenly home-sick. It does happen. Then he comes straight back to Hawks High to recharge his batteries, though this time, he tells me, there is another reason. He has agreed to give an interview to one of the glossy magazines. I forget which one. The reporter and photographer will be joining us some time this week. They're doing an 'in depth' interview, whatever that may mean."

Holly grasped eagerly at the information. "I see. Then Michael and I must be out of the way. It will probably be best if we go back to Sussex. Goodness knows how long it will take to repair the lodge."

Sir Matthew regarded her blandly, a slight smile on his fleshy pink face. "You will do nothing of the sort, my dear. I wouldn't hear of it. I'm only too delighted to have such charming company, and if I can give you a real holiday — which I understand is what you need — then it will be my pleasure."

"My aunt . . . " Holly faltered. "Has she talked about me?"

"Often. Yes, indeed, Mrs Dailie and I are old friends and she has told me of her great concern for you. Having met you, I share that concern. You are much too pale, my dear. You need a rest. I hope you will make yourself at home here at Hawks High. With good food and fresh air we shall soon put some colour back into your cheeks."

"Oh, but . . . " Holly began, horrified.

"No buts," Sir Matthew interrupted. He was smiling but there was a glint of determination in his eyes. "I am too much alone here. My wife died some years ago and I have no children, nor shall I have any grandchildren. Allow me to indulge myself spoiling yourself and your son. I shall be bitterly offended if you refuse."

It was a very generous offer, but Holly founds herself almost choking over her coffee. Sir Matthew didn't know what he was asking. To stay here, in the same house as Eden, in constant terror that her secret might be revealed? Oh, no!

"Everyone deserves a little luxury once in a while," Sir Matthew was saying. "You wouldn't be so foolish as to refuse, now would you?"

"You're very kind . . . " Holly found herself blurting, and the matter was settled.

She had been charmingly, disarmingly, trapped!

3

THERE was a breeze on the hillside, just enough to take the worst heat out of the sun. Holly lay among the bracken, watching Michael play some game with an invisible companion. After half an hour's energetic rolling down the hill, Holly was dishevelled and hot, but her son's energy was boundless.

"Mummy!" Michael called excitedly from way above her. "Look at me, Mummy. I'm at the top!"

Alarmed, Holly sat up, looking full into the sun as she lifted her eyes to the top of the steep slope behind her. Michael was up there, laughing and jumping up and down, waving his arms.

Fright shot through her as she scrambled to her feet. "Michael! Come down!"

45

Instead, he dodged away, out of her sight. With her mind full of the hidden dangers which might lie beyond the summit, Holly climbed after him, clinging to the bracken, calling his name.

She heard his laughter, but the boy remained out of sight and when she reached the top there was silence, no sign of her son. The breeze blew across a great expanse of dark purple heather.

"Michael!" There was fear in her voice now, which turned to anger when she heard his giggle and found him hiding in a shallow depression, but she swallowed the harsh words which sprang to her lips. Michael was only playing and the dangers were not so great.

"Come here, rascal!" She swept him high into the air before holding him safely in her arms. His sturdy limbs were warm from the sun and for a moment she was on the verge of tears as a wave of fierce protective love swept through her.

From that height on the hill she could see the house below, the valley stretching out beyond the gap where the road ran. Either side of it the hills ran up to the moor and to the right was the green of the larger dale where Beck Lodge was hidden.

Holly took a deep breath of the clear air. She could smell the fresh dampness of the land. How she loved the wild, unpredictable moors and the sheltered dales with their grey houses.

The moment was interrupted by the sound of an engine. Holly glanced down into the hollow and her tension returned, for it was Eden's black Jaguar which emerged from the cleft in the rocks and swung round to park in front of the big house below.

Sighing to herself, she carried Michael to the slope, intending to walk down with him. But from that angle it looked much too steep.

There was nothing for it but to sit down and edge through the bracken.

"I can do it," Michael complained,

wriggling from her grasp. She tried to retain his hand but he was too quick, sliding and rolling down the hill, then running the last stretch fearlessly.

Chagrined, Holly continued her own undignified descent. She was halfway down before she realised that Eden had not gone into the house but was standing watching her, one hand shading his eyes, the other wrapped firmly round Michael's small hand. The sight brought sickness broiling up from her stomach. They looked so right together, the tall, dark man and the small, dark boy. Dear God, how could she stand to remain at Hawks High?

"Do you want some help?" Eden's voice came across the intervening space, but even from that distance she could hear the amusement in it. He added something to Michael, whose clear laugh smote at Holly's heart.

Sheer perversity made her push herself to her feet, determined not to display her cowardice for Eden's

48

scorn. She placed her feet carefully, arms out for balance, then one foot slipped and to save herself she had to run, plunging madly downwards.

At the bottom, momentum carried her on, straight into Eden's waiting arms. The collision knocked the breath from her as she felt herself being whirled round and set securely on her feet, held tightly against him. She was aware of hard muscles and bare skin where his shirt was open to the waist, and though he only held her for a moment it was enough to set her blood pulsating wildly.

Scarlet-faced, she threw back her head to glare at him, seeing his face set, the black eyes sparking.

"What are you trying to do?" he demanded. "Break your neck?"

"I could have managed perfectly well!" she retorted.

"Oh, yes, it looked like it! Your son's got more sense than you have, you little idiot!"

Her heart had almost regained its

normal beat, though Eden's proximity kept it a little jerky. Feeling more in control of herself, she again dare a look at his face.

"How's my aunt?"

"Fine." His expression was shuttered now. "The neighbours are rallying round. She said I was to thank you for your offer of help, but it would be better if you stayed away for the moment. I told her I'd entertain you."

"I don't need entertaining!" Holly said sharply. "I shall be perfectly happy walking, and perhaps giving Mrs Grimson a hand."

He drew an angry breath. "You'll do nothing of the kind. You're a guest here."

"Only through force of circumstance. I'm used to housework."

"Oh, of course." His eyes narrowed in his hard-boned face and he thrust his thumbs into his belt. "You've been a housewife for . . . how long?"

"Almost five years," Holly lied flatly, looking round to check on Michael,

50

who was swinging round one of the verandah posts.

"How old is he?" Eden asked, following her gaze.

"Four — that is, almost four." Fresh spots of colour bloomed on her cheeks as she told the lie. But Eden could count, so she had to pretend that Michael was a few months younger than his real age.

"He's a beautiful boy," he remarked. "You're lucky. His father must have been proud of him."

"Yes." The words almost choked her. "Yes, he was."

Eden turned to look at her, black eyes thoughtful. "Sad memories?"

"What do you think?" Holly countered, and began to walk away, suppressing the urge to run. To her distress there were tears burning behind her eyes as she scooped Michael up and made swiftly for her room. On no account must she get into a discussion about Michael's father with Eden.

In the dining room, Sir Matthew was

51

helping himself to sherry. He offered Holly a glass, which she accepted.

"Would you prefer Michael to eat in the kitchen again?" she asked, glancing at the table where only three places were set.

"Not at all," the old man replied genially. "I told Mrs Grimson to let him eat with us. I'm hoping to get acquainted with him."

"But . . . isn't your nephew joining us?"

"Not today. He's gone off into town. Some shopping he had to do. Sit down, Mrs Hastings."

Perhaps, Holly thought, Eden had decided to avoid her, and if that was so then she was only too pleased with the arrangement.

After the meal, Sir Matthew took Michael's hand and led them on a tour of the ground floor, Holly trailing behind. Most of the time he talked to Michael, even lifting him up to stroke the nose of one of the stags' heads on the wall, so that Holly felt sorry that the old man had lost his own son. He would never know the joy of grandchildren and Eden showed no sign of producing any great-nieces or nephews for his uncle.

What was she thinking! Sir Matthew was holding his great-nephew by the hand right at that moment! It was something she had never considered before — that she had robbed Sir Matthew of his true relationship to Michael — but its impact made her feel dizzy.

The tour concluded, she took Michael up to his room for his afternoon nap and herself lay down in her underslip. She had intended only to rest until Michael woke, but the softness of the bed and the coolness of the room could not be denied and her long-fought weariness gave in to their seduction.

A sharp tapping on her door reached down into her sleep and she came awake with a guilty start, calling, "Yes?"

To her horror, the opening door

revealed Eden standing eyebrow crooked mockingly as he let his eyes wander over her, making Holly hotly aware of her undressed state, the slip riding above her knees. One lacy strap had fallen down her arm. She furiously dragged it back into place and reached for a pillow, to hug it defensively in front of her.

"How dare you walk in here?" she demanded, green eyes glazing in her flaming face.

"I haven't just walked in," Eden replied. "I'm only on the threshold. Though I'll put that right."

He bent to pick up something from the floor of the hall and Holly leapt to her feet with some wild idea about slamming the door, but before she could cross the carpet Eden was coming in, his arms full of packages. Anger and embarrassment warred with her curiosity, but the former won and she fled into the bathroom, where she flung on her long bathrobe. Pulling the pink towelling securely around her, she clinched the belt and returned to the bedroom prepared for a showdown.

The packages were strewn across the crumpled coverlet and beside them Eden Pemberley sat, one foot on the opposite knee, arms braced behind him on the bed in such a way that his unbuttoned shirt was pulled open to reveal more of his muscular chest. It was a consciously provocative pose, lazy and yet aggressive, as if he belonged there.

Tiny prickles broke out on Holly's skin, summoned by apprehension. To cover her fear, she lifted her chin and spoke coldly.

"Just what do you think you're doing?"

"Sitting on your bed," he answered sardonically. "What does it look like?"

"I mean, why have you come? Michael's only in the next room, you know."

Eden shook his head, a brief, confident smile curving his mouth. "Good try, my dear Mrs Hastings, but

I've just seen your son — downstairs with my uncle. However, to answer your question, the purpose of my mission must be apparent." A nod of the head indicated the scattered packages, which looked puzzlingly like dress boxes and carrier bags from various ladies' outfitters. "Consider me to be Paris," Eden added, "bringing tributes to fair Helen."

"I always understood that one had to beware of Greeks bearing gifts," Holly retorted, hoping he couldn't see that she was trembling. One hand held the edges of her robe tightly to her throat.

Throwing back his head, Eden laughed aloud and suddenly stood up, smiling at her. The smile was not a pleasant one. "Paris was a Trojan, not a Greek. However, the sentiment may be right. But you don't need to be told to be wary, do you? You're very much on your guard."

"Do you blame me?" she shot at him.

"It mystifies me. What exactly have I done to be treated like a pariah? If I was abrupt this morning, put it down to tiredness. One moves through several time-zones on the flight from California. It tends to upset the equilibrium."

"Jet-lag, you mean?" Holly said with sarcasm. "You blame a lot of things on to that, don't you? What excuse do you use when you haven't been travelling?" She turned away, catching sight of the packages on the bed. "And whatever these are, you can . . . you can take them away, and yourself with them!"

"That would be ridiculous," he argued, the dry note of mockery still in his voice. "They are for you — a small token of my uncle's esteem. He wants you to feel at home here, and your aunt told me your wardrobe is limited. Since we are about to have other visitors, you will no doubt want to create a good impression."

Feeling sick, Holly glared at him. "Other visitors?"

"Some people from 'Galaxy' magazine."

"And you seriously think I would accept presents from your uncle, just to impress them? Surely Sir Matthew knew that . . . "

"He wouldn't think beyond his own pleasure in giving," Eden interrupted levelly. "Wear the things to please him. There are more in the next room — for your son, who is at this moment playing with a train set which I also brought. If you won't use them, they'll only go to waste."

She swallowed the shame in her throat, saying thickly, "Is this why you went into town? For this? Didn't it occur to you that I might feel insulted by such. . . "

"Of course it occurred to me," Eden said smoothly.

"Then why didn't you explain it to your uncle?"

Dark eyebrows rose high over wide, seeming-innocent black eyes. "And spoil his fun? He has few pleasures left in life, my dear Mrs Hastings. And

58

besides . . . " He paused, the wicked spark back in his eyes.

"Besides what?"

"It amused me," he told her, lips twitching. "I wanted to see what you would do. Will you be foolish enough to refuse this generous gift? Your husband obviously omitted to provide for you. Why throw back such a windfall? Is it pride?"

"Sometimes pride is all a person has!" Holly retaliated. "You probably wouldn't understand that. Or perhaps you do. Perhaps it amuses you to rob me of that, too. Why do you enjoy baiting me, Eden? Hasn't enough harm been done already?"

Only when she noted the puzzlement on his face did she realise that she had allowed anger to take away her caution.

"Harm?" he repeated curiously. "What harm?"

Frantically, Holly cast around for some answer apart from the true one that a child had been brought into the world fatherless, that her life had been altered for the worse and her emotions shredded. "Nothing," she said flatly. "Just leave me alone, can't you? I never wanted to come here. You should never have brought me."

His expression had changed, darkening into a scowl. "That's the thanks I get, is it?" He stepped towards her and she instinctively drew back, arms thrown protectively across herself.

Eden stopped almost in mid-stride, hanging there with every muscle tensed, his face grim and his body alert. "What are you afraid of, Holly? Do you think I might attempt to seduce you again?"

"At least you admit it was seduction!" she flung back.

"I admit nothing," Eden snarled, clenching his teeth so that a muscle jumped in his jaw. "I don't recall forcing myself on you. I seem to remember you were entirely willing. Exactly who are you afraid of? Me, or yourself? Could I do it again if I tried?"

"No!" She was shaking with fear, backed up so far she could feel the wall behind her. "No, you certainly could not! Come one step nearer and I'll scream the place down. I warn you, Eden . . . "

With an angry gesture, he whirled on his heel and strode from the room, slamming the door behind him with such force that a picture on the wall trembled on its nail. Holly, too, was trembling, herself supported by the wall. It was true, she thought wretchedly. If he tried to make love to her it would all happen again. She had no defences against the sensual power of him.

Another knock on the door announced the arrival of Mrs Grimson, with a tea tray. She intended to give Michael his tea in the kitchen, she said. Dinner would be at seven thirty, when Mrs Dailie was expected to join the party.

"My aunt?" Holly was relieved. "Oh, good. I didn't realise she was coming."

Mrs Grimson put down the tray on

the ottoman, her eyes flicking over the debris on the bed before returning to Holly's dishevelled hair and pale face.

"I met Mr Eden on the stairs," she remarked.

"Oh, yes, he . . . he brought me these things, though I don't intend to accept them. Does Sir Matthew lavish gifts on everyone he knows?"

"He's a very generous man," was the enigmatic answer. "He's taken a real liking to you and your little boy. Why, you should have seen the two of them, playing with that train. They looked a picture Mrs Hastings . . . It's not my place to say this, but I should be a bit careful of Mr Eden if I were you. He's a very physical man. It wouldn't be wise to let him in your room."

"I don't think you need worry about that," Holly said coolly.

Although she had no thought of keeping the gifts, she was curious to see what Eden had brought and tipped the contents of one carrier bag on to the counterpane. Her lips tightened grimly at the sight of shimmering pastel underwear. No wonder Eden had been 'amused' at the thought of her reaction. Even though she was alone her face burned at the thought of him choosing these things for her.

They were just the kind of clothes Holly had always longed to wear. She had to admit that Eden had good taste. But there was no way she could ever wear any of these things.

Remembering that Eden had said he had similarly supplied Michael, she hurried through into the smaller room and discovered there a complete new wardrobe for her son.

She threw the clothes down and sat on the bed, distressed. If he had wanted to prove how inadequately she could provide for her son, he could not have done it any surer way than this. It was not only insulting. It was cruel!

4

LEAVING the new clothes where they were flung over the two beds, Holly drank tea and ate some of the thin sandwiches Mrs Grimson had brought, then donned her own green cotton dress and took the tray down to the kitchen. Michael and the housekeeper were both seated at the table in the big, airy room.

"Mummy!" Michael cried, rushing to throw his arms round Holly's legs. "Mummy, I've got a train. Come and see."

"Finish your tea first, darling," she said in a strained voice. "Mrs Grimson, where is Sir Matthew at the moment?"

"Out on the verandah getting some air," the housekeeper replied.

Walking through the dark hall with its grisly trophies of bygone hunts, Holly emerged on to the verandah with her shoulders squared determined not to be bested. Sir Matthew sat in a cane chair beside a small table, and to Holly's irritation Eden was also there, his long legs stretched across the verandah.

"Come and join us!" Sir Matthew invited, beaming from beneath the brim of a large straw hat. "Did you have a good rest? Mrs Grimson heard Michael was awake, so she brought him down. He and I have been enjoying ourselves."

"Yes, so I've heard. Sir Matthew . . ."

"Well, sit down, my dear. Sit down and enjoy the breeze. It's pleasant now the sun has moved round. Not so hot."

It would have been easier to have said what she wanted to say from a standing position, but with a stifled sigh she perched on the hard edge of the vacant chair next to the old man. "Sir Matthew . . ."

"Eden tells me you think I have over-reached myself," he broke in with a grin. "If you're going to protest, save yourself the trouble. I hope Eden's choice meets with your approval?"

"Yes, but . . . " She spoke slowly, choosing her words with care. "If you wish to give to deserving cases, there are people in greater need than I. I do appreciate the thought, but . . . "

"Then that is all I ask," he interrupted for the third time, smiling implacably. "Indulge me, Holly. May I call you Holly? It's a pretty name, though strangely inappropriate for someone so young and tender. Holly ought by rights to have prickles."

Eden's voice came slow and mocking. "How do you know she hasn't got prickles, uncle Matthew?"

"Oh, Eden will have his little joke!" the old man said merrily, patting Holly's arm. "Take no notice of him, my dear."

That was exactly what she had been trying to do, but Eden's presence could not be ignored. A glance at him assured Holly that he had not been joking. He watched her from beneath lowered lids, with an inscrutable expression, dark-faced and enigmatic.

"I won't hear another word," Sir Matthew was saying. "You will wear the clothes to please me. Your son isn't so proud. He was delighted with the train set. Believe me, the pleasure is entirely mine. I do adore having beautiful young women around me."

"I still don't understand why you're being so generous to me." Holly protested. "You don't know the first thing about me. I might be a . . . a fortune hunter, or something."

Sir Matthew laughed. "Nonsense, my dear. I'm a better judge of character than that. Your aunt has talked so much about you, I feel I have known you for a long time."

At that moment the front door opened and Michael rushed out, demanding that Holly come and see his train set. She was not sorry to leave the verandah.

The train set, fortunately, was only

a simple affair with a small circle of rail round which the battery-driven engine shunted happily. It was laid out around one of the occasional tables in the big sitting room.

Holly sat on the floor while Michael showed her how the train worked. His uncomplicated delight in his new toy made Holly feel mean for wanting to deprive him of this pleasure, though she was still unsure that she ought to allow Sir Matthew to "indulge" himself in this way.

"Well!" Their host came in, smiling at the scene before him. "Isn't it a fine train, Michael? There are one or two books here, too, Holly. If you will allow me, I shall enjoy reading them to him." He sat down in an armchair, one hand briefly touching Michael's curls.

"You're too kind, Sir Matthew," Holly said awkwardly.

Fixing her with bright, bland eyes, he teased, "Can one be too kind? Perhaps I'm preparing my way to heaven. Seriously, Holly, I feel brighter than I have done in months, having you and Michael here."

"Might it not be that your nephew is home?" she asked.

"That, too, I don't doubt. My dear, I hope you will make allowances for Eden. He seems to be upset about something. He says it's only the effects of the long journey, but I have a feeling there is more behind it — something he won't discuss with me. He hinted that he may not be returning to the States, and from the way he said it I rather gathered that it is there the trouble lies. A young woman, perhaps. Who knows?"

Aware that she had no right to comment, Holly watched the train rattle round the track and told herself that the pang she felt was not jealousy.

"I believe his wife's death affected him more than he cares to admit," Sir Matthew confided. "Not her death, exactly, but the manner of it. She was drowned, you know." He nodded sombrely. "Unfortunately the police got it into their heads that Eden was somehow implicated, though anyone who knows Eden would know that he is incapable of a crime like that. Besides, if he had wanted to be rid of Lucy, he could easily have divorced her."

Unable to stop herself, Holly asked, "Did he want to be rid of her?"

"As to that . . . " He scratched his bald head, sighing. "I really don't know. From the little I saw of it, they weren't suited, but . . ."

"You're very fond of him, aren't you?" Holly said softly.

The old man sighed, smiled. "Indeed I am. He is all I have left. I tend to worry about him — too much, so he says, but with little else to occupy my mind it is difficult not to worry. That's why I'm so glad to have you and your son here for a short while. It gives me another interest."

Holly understood perfectly. She was drawn to the benign old man who, for all his wealth, was lonely and unhappy.

Later, she bathed Michael and put him into his pyjamas. The new clothes had all been put away in drawers and wardrobe — presumably by Mrs Grimson — and Holly discarded the last lingering doubt about the wisdom of accepting them. It was a virtue to be a gracious recipient as well as a gracious giver and she knew that Sir Matthew would be hurt if she made more protests.

She read Michael a story from one of his own books and, leaving him to drift into sleep, went to her own room to prepare for dinner. She was tempted to wear one of the new dresses, but Sir Matthew had said that informality was the usual rule at Hawks High so she decided to keep on her own green cotton. Besides, her aunt might be shocked at the idea of Holly accepting gifts, and Jo would certainly not dress up.

Summoned by Grimson, who informed her that her aunt had arrived, Holly finished brushing out her hair, checked that Michael was asleep, and hurried down to see Jo, eager to hear about Beck Lodge. But as she ran down the stairs Eden emerged from the passageway and stood watching her with a cynical smile on his face. His casual shirt and slacks had been replaced by a beige safari suit and an open-necked shirt in a brilliant orange that showed up his deep tan.

"Still retaining your independence?" he queried with a gesture at her attire. "You disappoint me, Holly. Aren't you woman enough to enjoy new clothes?"

"And careful enough to keep them for the right occasion," she returned. "I understood we were not expected to dress for dinner."

"Then maybe we should undress," he said under his breath.

Stiffening, Holly made to sweep past him, but he caught her arm, saying, "Have you really got so prudish? I was joking."

"I'm afraid I don't find your jokes very amusing," she said haughtily lifting her head to look him in the eye.

"You used to," Eden said in a low voice, his eyes resting on her mouth so that tiny beads of sweat burst on her skin.

Again she was tremblingly aware of the effect his nearness produced in her, her senses all alert to him, and where his hand rested on her bare arm the flesh seemed alive, responding to his warm touch all on its own.

"That was a long time ago," she replied coldly, though her voice was hoarse. "A great deal has happened to us both. We're different people now."

"Ah, yes," he sighed, his mouth twisting. "The fabulous Mr Hastings, of course. What was his first name?"

"Is that any business of yours?" Holly countered, vainly trying to release the grip on her arm.

"I would have thought it was a fair question," Eden said. "He must have had a first name."

"It was — Peter," she blurted, suddenly unable to think of any other name. "Eden, please let me go!"

His fingers unlocked at once, releasing her. "Of course, my dear Mrs Hastings," he taunted. "You had only to ask."

"And stop calling me your dear Mrs Hastings!" Holly raged.

A black eyebrow quirked quizzically. "It's your name, isn't it?"

The question brought a fresh pang of dismay. "Of course it's my name!" she cried. "But I am not yours and you've made it very clear that I'm not dear to you." Whirling away from him, she swung towards the safety of the sitting room.

With relief she saw that her aunt was there with Sir Matthew. Holly almost ran across the room, mostly to greet Jo warmly but also partly to escape from Eden.

"Aunt Jo! How are you?"

"Very well, my dear, thank you. Busy, of course, but then hard work never bothered me."

As Holly had guessed, Jo had not troubled to wear anything special for the dinner party. Her straight dress was made of grey jersey, several years old. A wave of tenderness swept through Holly. Dear Aunt Jo. She was always severely herself, whatever the circumstances.

"What about the house?" Holly asked anxiously. "Is there very much damage?"

"Nothing that can't be mended," was the brisk reply. "They're coming tomorrow to cut up the tree and the power should be reconnected in a day or two. Give me a couple of weeks and the place will be back to normal."

A couple of weeks! Holly thought in agitation, though the arrival of Sir Matthew with a glass of sherry allowed her to cover the emotion. One thing she was thankful for was that Jo seemed to be coping with the disaster in her usual businesslike fashion.

"Of course," she was saying, "you'll be able to come back sooner than that. Once I've got electricity . . ."

"But you must be sure the place is

safe," Sir Matthew put in anxiously. "You can't risk the house coming down about your ears."

"I hardly think there's any danger of that," Jo replied. "It's very kind of you to have Holly and Michael here, Sir Matthew, but in a couple of days they can come back to me."

"So soon?" There was an almost wistful air about the old man. "But you'll be busy, won't you? Cleaning up and so forth? Don't rush it on my account I'm only too delighted to have Holly and her son here. We both are." He turned and spoke across the room. "Aren't we, Eden?"

Eden had remained by the cocktail cabinet, where he was pouring himself a second generous whisky. He bowed slightly, waving the bottle in the air. "Enchanted," he said flatly.

Grimson appeared to announce that dinner was served and Sir Matthew offered Jo his arm. Walking behind them, Holly was aware of Eden crossing the room with a pantherish stride, his glass in one hand.

"Allow me, my dear Mrs Hastings," he drawled, giving her a mocking but courtly bow as he extended his arm.

Holly wished she could have hit him, but since that was out of the question she gave him a tight false smile and laid her hand lightly in the crook of his elbow, trying to ignore the ripple of warm muscle beneath the linen of his jacket.

The four places had been arranged, widely-spaced, on either side of the long table. Holly had Sir Matthew on her right, opposite her aunt, and Eden strolled languidly round to arrange his long legs under the table across from her. She saw her aunt glance sharply from her face to Eden's, obviously aware that some undercurrent was racing beneath the polite and tranquil surface; so Holly smiled ingenuously, as if nothing at all was wrong.

Sir Matthew and Jo made most of the conversation, while Holly tried to force down her food. When the main course was served she accepted a portion but refused vegetables.

"Aren't you hungry?" Eden demanded, forcing her to look at him for the first time since they had sat down. "Good heavens, girl, no wonder you're like a wraith."

"I had some sandwiches earlier," Holly said.

"Sandwiches!" Eden repeated derisively and would have gone on but for a pleading "Eden!" from his uncle, which made him subside momentarily before adding, "I was under the impression she had come to Yorkshire to build herself up. From the looks of her, she was desperately in need of this holiday."

"She was," Jo agreed. "Holly has had a bad time lately, what with her grandfather's death — and her husband's."

"Both at once?" Sir Matthew enquired, concerned. "Oh, my dear . . . "

Holly was staring at her plate, wondering why Jo had had to bring the sticky subject up at just that moment. "My . . . my husband died last year," she announced. "And then, this spring, I lost my grandfather. We had been living with him at the farm."

"What happened to your husband?" Eden wanted to know.

"Eden . . . " his uncle protested. "You're being very inconsiderate."

"Oh, there's no mystery about it," Jo Dailie put in. "There was a road accident. He crashed his car. Of course it was a terrible shock to Holly. They had been so happy. And poor little Michael will never know his father. He doesn't even remember him."

"Tragic," said Sir Matthew sorrowfully. "Tragic."

Suddenly Holly wanted to run from the room. It was intolerable that she should be obliged to lie to the old man after all his kindness.

"More wine?" Eden offered, and when she refused he filled his own glass for a third time.

Holly surreptitiously watched his

throat work as he swallowed, her eyes going to the glimpse of gold chain round his neck, which disappeared behind his orange shirt. Then Eden's fingers came up and unfastened another button of his shirt, and when Holly glanced up, startled, he gave her a slow sensuous smile which made her thoughts dart round her head like bats in a cave.

Under cover of a burst of laughter from the two older people, Eden leaned across the table to say in a low, jibing voice, "You look like a frightened faun, my dear Mrs Hastings."

He asked permission to smoke and lit a thin cigar, glancing through curls of smoke at Holly. The match flame threw twin reflections in his eyes. He seemed amused, but in the depths of his narrowed gaze there was something cold, something dangerous, and when he snapped the match in half with one flick of his fingers, Holly winced. The simple act was like a threat, as if he was reminding her that he could as easily snap her delicate bones.

Stop it! She told herself sharply. Holly West, your imagination has gone into overdrive. Holly West . . . I am Holly West, not Holly Hastings. I want to stand up and announce the fact.

Sir Matthew suggested that they should have coffee in the sitting room and once again he escorted Jo, leaving Eden to hold the door politely for Holly. She avoided his eyes as she passed.

"Holly!" His voice, low and urgent, stopped her in the centre of the hall.

Without turning, she stiffened, her hands clenched so tight that her nails cut into her. "Leave me alone, Eden."

"But I have something to show you," he said, coming beside her and reaching into his shirt for the gold medallion which hung on the chain. He held it out on his palm for her to see. "It's a Spanish doubloon, from one of the sunken treasure ships in the Caribbean. Feel the weight of it."

Gingerly, Holly lifted the coin, being

careful not to touch his hand, and turned it over to look at the reverse side, her tumble of hair only inches from his face.

"Still warm, isn't it?" Eden murmured. "From being next to my skin."

She dropped the coin as if it had burned her, throwing her head back to look at him. "Must you be so . . . so . . . "

"So what?" Eden asked, wide-eyed. "I was about to show you this at the table, but from the look you gave me . . . Whatever did you think I intended?"

"I thought what you intended me to think!" Holly said angrily.

"What? Am I hypnotist now?"

"Oh . . . leave me alone!"

As she turned away, her aunt emerged from the sitting room, to glance speculatively at them both.

"I thought we could go and check on Michael," she said, and Holly was relieved to go with her, away from Eden's disturbing presence.

Michael was deeply asleep, his teddy clutched in one arm. When both women had dropped light kisses on his forehead, Holly led the way into her own room. She knew her aunt wanted to talk to her.

Outside the light was fading, leaving purple shadows to mist in the hollows, and through the open window there came the raucous cry of a grouse.

"It's a pity you can't see across the moor," Holly said, leaning out of the window. "Isn't this a lovely room, Aunt Jo?"

"Lovely," Jo said, her tone so flat that Holly turned in surprise. "I think it's about time you told me exactly what is going on," Jo added crisply. "And don't pretend you don't know what I mean. Are you still attracted to him?"

"To whom?" Holly gasped, startled by the sudden attack.

"Well, I'm not talking about Sir Matthew!" Jo snapped. "I knew it was a mistake to let you come, but at the time there was no alternative. I thought you had grown out of that silly infatuation."

"I have," Holly said quietly.

"Then what is it between you? Don't tell me there's nothing because I didn't just fall off the Christmas tree. If you haven't been mooning after him like a sixteen-year-old, what have you done to annoy him?"

"Annoy him?" Holly echoed in amazement. "Nothing at all. Aunt Jo . . . forgive me, but I wish you wouldn't speak to me as if I were a child."

Jo ran a hand through her short hair sinking down on the ottoman at the foot of the bed. "I'm sorry, but I feel responsible for you, and I know what a reputation on Eden Pemberley has. I'm not so old I can't see his attractions, you know."

"Physical attractions," Holly qualified. "And I'm no longer a novice in such matters." She was trembling, her hands clenched tightly on the windowsill, because no matter how she denied it, aloud or in her head, the fact was that Eden still exercised some mystical power over her. Even when he was mocking her, still something within her cried out to him in agony, longing for the tenderness she remembered so vividly.

5

THE bleating of sheep woke Holly from muddled dreams. A warm breeze stirred the curtains, allowing the sunlight to peep into the room, and she stretched luxuriously, feeling really rested for the first time in weeks. Probably the clean air had worked the miracle.

Possibly, also, Eden's absence the previous evening had enabled her to relax. When she and Jo had returned to the sitting room for coffee, Sir Matthew had informed them that Eden had decided to have an early night.

But where was Michael? The single bed in the next room was empty, with Michael's pyjamas neatly folded and the covers thrown back to air the bed. Only then did Holly think to look at her watch and found to her horror that it was ten o'clock. On the bedside table a cup of coffee had grown cold.

Feeling guilty, Holly took a quick shower and threw on some clothes. Even before she reached the stairs she heard Michael 'choo-chooing' to the buzz of his engine, which was trundling across the hall, off its rails. Michael scrambled beside it, while Sir Matthew stood in the sitting room doorway, smiling happily at the absorbed child.

"Good morning," he greeted as Holly came down the stairs. "We thought it would do you good to sleep in. Look, Michael, here's Mummy."

"Hello, Mummy," said Michael, not even glancing up. Then he threw himself round in excitement to add, "Look at my new suit! Uncle . . ." With a frown he looked at the old man.

"Matthew," Eden's uncle said with a smile.

"Yes," agreed Michael. "Uncle Maffew gave it to me. And lots of more things. And my train!"

"I know," Holly said with a catch in

her voice. "Sir Matthew is very kind." So he had become 'uncle,' had he? She was being drawn into an inextricable tangle, very much against her will.

Sir Matthew rang for Grimson and ordered coffee, while Holly seated herself in a corner of the big settee. At least, she thought relievedly, there was no sign of Eden. Maybe he had gone out.

"Eden was up early," Sir Matthew said, flopping into an armchair. "He's gone riding. He said he had slept well, which is a good sign. One can't cope with emotional problems when one is tired."

"Emotional problems?" Holly queried.

"The woman — or whatever it was that made him leave America so hurriedly."

Grimson arrived with the coffee, bringing a glass of milk for Michael, who downed the drink in a series of gulps and rushed back to his train.

"He's having a fine time." Sir Matthew beamed. "What a charming little fellow he is, my dear. I hope, when you return to Beck Lodge, you will come frequently to visit me, and keep in touch when you return to Sussex?"

"I'll be glad to." Holly sipped her coffee, glancing out of the tall windows at the hollow where a group of sheep wandered. "It's a lovely day again."

"It is," her host agreed, wrily noticing the change of subject. "Well! We shall be having more visitors this afternoon. Those magazine people will be here later."

"Today?" she asked in surprise.

"Apparently so. The reporter intends to stay for a few days — to interview Eden 'in depth' — which probably means at great length, so that he can then pick out the most startling bits for publication."

His tone was derisory and Holly laughed. "You don't sound very fond of newspaper people, Sir Matthew."

"Indeed I am not, having been misquoted several times."

"Did Eden consult you before he arranged this invasion?"

"Only after it had been arranged. This is, after all, his home and he is free to invite whoever he chooses, though I must admit it puzzled me. Usually he would do anything to avoid giving an interview. I only hope this reporter has a thick skin. If Eden's temper remains as uncertain as it has been for these last two days the man may find his notebook being rammed down his throat."

The reporter, Holly thought, might become the target for Eden's sardonic humour, which would provide a respite for her. The notion brought a sharp pang of disappointment to surprise her. She had only a few more days to spend Hawks high. If Eden was going to be occupied during the whole of that time . . . She angrily stamped on the thought, telling herself she didn't care if she never saw Eden again.

Sir Matthew departed to write some letters and Holly, realising that Michael was very quiet, went in search of him. Very soon the search became worrying, for Michael was nowhere to be found in the house. But in the dining room the french doors stood open, making her panic. Dear God, the hills and the moor . . .

"Michael!" She ran along the verandah, past the sitting room windows. From there the east wing stretched out across the uneven grass, one end of it taken up by Eden's studio, which Sir Matthew had said was private.

Holly ran the length of the wing, scanning the curve of the hill, calling again, "Michael!"

The only answer came from a grouse, which scuttled from the bracken and took off with a clatter of wings. Or had there been another reply, a thin sound whose direction was unclear?

She shouted her son's name with rising fear, and this time a tapping sounded from behind her. Whirling, she saw Michael grinning through the glass of a large door. Behind him, dark blue curtains were drawn across as if to shut out the sun.

"Michael!" She was horrified. "What are you doing in there?"

Glancing at the front door, which seemed miles away, Holly reached for the handle above her son's head. Laughing, Michael ducked through the curtains and disappeared as the door came open.

Feeling flushed with guilt, Holly glanced round behind her. Thank goodness Eden had gone riding. She had no wish to be discovered in his studio, where even Mrs Grimson was not allowed when Eden was at home.

It was cool in the studio and would have been gloomy except that the curtains at the far window were pulled back, allowing a view of the sunny hill beyond. In the corner near where she stood, a single bed was roughly made. Next to it stood a dressing table scattered untidily with personal belongings, and then a big wardrobe. The centre of the huge room was empty but for Michael, who was running his train across the carpet.

It was studio, bedroom, lounge: a self-contained unit where Eden could work in private. The faint smell of his after-shave hung on the air, but there was no whiff of paint. Of course, Eden had been in America for a long time.

"My train's stopped!" Michael complained, bringing the engine for Holly to see.

"You've probably worn it out," she said. "How did you get in here, Michael?"

He pointed to the open door in the side wall. "The train comed all down there and frough the door."

"Then you should have taken it back! You're a naughty boy!"

He frowned at her, mouth drooping sulkily, dark eyes glaring accusingly through thick lashes. "I want my train to go!"

"It would serve you right if it never went again!" Holly scolded. "Let me see." Taking the train, she noticed how

93

grubby his hands were. "You need a good wash, young man."

Glowering, Michael sat down on the floor with a bump.

As far as Holly could see, there was nothing wrong with the toy except that the battery was flat.

"You must have left it switched on last night," she told her son. "You'll have to play with something else until . . . "

She stopped, frozen into immobility as the sun poured in from behind her and a shadow fell across the carpet by her feet.

"Isn't anything sacred?" Eden's voice said tightly.

Holly whirled to face him, the engine clutched in one hand while the other wiped itself nervously down her cords. Eden was dressed for riding. Beyond him Holly glimpsed the gleaming flank of a horse, but her eyes were fixed on the craggy face beneath the unruly tumble of dark hair and her heart was jolting uncontrollably.

"I'm afraid Michael wandered in here," she blurted. "I was just going to remove him."

Eden looked at the child, who was still sitting on the floor moodily banging his heels. "What's wrong with him? What's the matter, Michael?"

"My train got broked," Michael said sullenly.

"It isn't broken!" Holly exclaimed. "Eden, I'm sorry. It wasn't my intention to pry. I swear to you . . . "

She was stopped by the spark of impatience in his eyes. He held out his hand. "Let me look at the train."

Relinquishing it, Holly stepped away and saw Eden reach into his shirt pocket and bring out — astonishingly — a new battery. He squatted down in front of Michael, ejecting the old power unit.

"I had a feeling that might happen," he said to the child, his voice more friendly than Holly had yet heard it. "So I stopped at the shop and got a couple more. Shall we see if it works?"

Michael nodded excitedly, kneeling up to put one small hand on the man's tanned wrist, the two dark heads bent in concentration over the toy. Swallowing a sob, Holly turned away, everything in her tensed against the tears that threatened.

"Switch it on, then," Eden urged, and the buzz of the engine's motor sounded like an angry bee in the still room.

"Hooray!" Michael yelled.

Holly looked round, seeking refuge in stern maternalism. "And what else, Michael?"

After blinking at her, understanding dawned on the child's face and he flung his arms round Eden's neck, kissing the lean brown cheek. "Thank you!" he shouted gaily. "My train's all better!" and scampered away to let the train run on the expanse of carpet.

Holly's eyes were wide with pain as she watched Eden stretch to his full height, one hand touching his face where her son's lips had rested briefly. Her son — his son — their son. There was puzzlement in his face as he watched the child.

Stricken, Holly wondered what he was seeing. The likeness . . . ?

"That was awfully kind of you," she babbled nervously. "I'll have to make sure he switches it off properly in future. Well . . . I'll leave you in peace."

"Running away, are you, Holly?" he asked drily, making her eyes snap back to his face.

"Not at all." There was an annoying croak in her voice. "Your uncle said you don't like people in here. If Michael hadn't . . . It's my fault for not watching him. He's beginning to feel at home here, I'm afraid."

"He's different from you, then," Eden commented. "You don't feel at home here, do you? Isn't it comfortable? Aren't you being treated as an honoured guest?"

"Your uncle is being extremely

courteous," she replied, and her head snapped round as she heard Michael run from the room, leaving her alone with Eden. "Michael!"

"Let him go," Eden said with a sharp laugh. "He's having fun. Why don't you relax, too?"

"Because I have to keep an eye on him. Excuse me."

She made a determined start towards the open door, but Eden strode after her, reached the door first and closed it, leaning against it with a sardonic smile.

"What if I won't excuse you?"

"Oh — stop playing with me!" The words burst from her in an anguished cry and she lifted her fists as if to strike him. "Eden . . . I'm so tired of this stupid battling. Why do you enjoy baiting me? Does it feed your ego? I'm no match at all. I don't have your biting talent for words. Please!" The small fists spread out in frank appeal. "I can't take any more."

Eden's face twisted. "Then shall we

talk about the weather, or the price of bread?"

"I don't care what we talk about, as long as it's something normal. Let's . . . let's talk about you. About your work. What are you engaged in at the moment?"

With a heavy sigh, Eden came away from the door and strolled to the centre of the room, stretching his shoulders as if they were aching. Holly watched him, half her mind on the now-available door, but Eden's words and the wide gesture which accompanied them brought her full attention back to the tall man.

"As you can plainly see, I'm engaged in no work at all," he said with a hopeless note in his deep voice.

Puzzled, Holly stepped towards him. "But in California . . . "

"Not in California. Not in New York, or Rio de Janeiro, or on the Mediterranean. Nothing!"

"Why?"

"Why?" He flung back his head and

99

sent a sharp, unhumorous laugh at the ceiling. "Aye, there's the rub! Would you believe my muse has deserted me?" The black eyes spitted her as if on a rapier's tip, glittering ironically.

"No, I wouldn't," Holly said flatly.

"Neither would I. There is no such thing as a muse, my dear Mrs Hastings. There is only hard work, application, dedication. But recently it has gone anaemic on me. I paint only rubbish. I am disgusted by it, and therefore . . . " He paused, his lips drawn back in a wolfish smile. "Therefore, my dear Mrs Hastings, I intend to quit."

The announcement stunned Holly. Eden Pemberley to stop painting? She could imagine the headlines, the speculation. But she was unsure whether to take him seriously.

"I see." She bit the words off as she spoke them. "So that's what the trouble is — self pity? I'm surprised at you, Eden."

As she had hoped, the thrust brought him off the stage and back to reality.

"Self-pity?" he snarled. "My God, Holly . . . "

"Well, what would you call it?" she demanded. "Perhaps you're jaded and need a rest. Perhaps you're just suffering from a temporary loss of confidence. It does happen, doesn't it?"

His face was as still as the carving on a totem pote, only his eyes alive, burning coldly. "What do you know about it?"

"I can read! You say your recent work is rubbish. Is it really, or have you lost your ability to judge? What about this?"

'This' was the canvas covered by the sheet. She swept across the room towards the easel, picked up a corner of the sheet — and gasped with pain as Eden's fingers bit into her wrist.

"You touch that and I'll break your neck!" he threatened in a low voice.

"Oh, yes!" She threw back her head, green eyes bright with anger. "That's about your level. Let go of my arm!

101

You're hurting me!"

"Then stop struggling," he said through his teeth. "That's better." But the hand remained locked about her arm so that she could not draw away. "It's odd, but I don't remember you being such a wildcat when we met before."

"And I don't recall you being so edgy," Holly returned. "What's happened to you, Eden?"

"I might ask you the same," he said, but the harshness was lifting from his face as he looked down at her.

Holly's skin vibrated under the scrutiny. For her sanity's sake, she wished he would not look at her like that. But she was encouraged by the softening of his mouth, enough to ask gently, "Was it your wife? Is that what's troubling you?"

Instantly his eyes transfixed hers with a furious glare and she felt his tension return, transmitting itself to her through the fingers held firmly round her wrist.

"My wife?" His voice was dangerously quiet. "What about her?"

"I . . . just wondered. Your uncle said you had a bad time, with the police and everything."

"I did." Now his tone had turned satirical. "It was natural enough, I suppose. Everyone knew that Lucy and I fought like cat and dog. She disliked me as much as I disliked her."

"Then why did you marry her?"

Eden laughed harshly. "I often wonder. Why did you marry Peter Hastings?"

The question was shot at her so abruptly that Holly was disconcerted. Because . . . because I loved him."

"Love!" He almost spat the word and his fingers tightened round her arm. He brought his face down until it was only inches from hers. "What I want to know, Holly," he said slowly and deliberately, "is when you met him."

"Met . . . ?" Holly faltered.

"Your husband! Did you meet him

before that summer or afterwards? Did you know him before you met me?"

"Eden . . . " Frantic, she glanced at the powerful hand locked round her arm, so tightly that the knuckles gleamed white.

"Answer me!" Eden snarled.

At that moment, Sir Matthew's voice called to him from just beyond the closed door. Eden froze, staring across the room.

"Eden, lunch is ready!" Sir Matthew called. "Is Holly there?"

"Yes," Eden replied. "We're coming."

Holly flinched away when he turned on her again. "You haven't answered my question. When did you meet Peter Hastings?"

Her wrist hurt abominably, but the pain brought temper to her aid. "I have known Peter Hastings since I was four years old!" There, that was the truth and he could take it how he liked, though it didn't answer the real question he was asking.

"Oh, it was a boy and girl thing, was

it?" Eden sneered. "How very cosy. Romping in the hay and so on. You really had me fooled."

"Yes, didn't I?" She was too angry now to care what he thought. "It was great — running rings round the fabulous Eden Pemberley! You're supposed to know so much about women. You know nothing!"

A thunderous frown brought the tangle of dark hair almost into eyes that glowed with uncontrollable fury.

"Go ahead and hit me!" Holly raged. "Is that what you did to Lucy? Did she puncture your over-inflated ego, too?"

"Lucy?" He stared at her as if she were a stranger. "My God! That, too? You believe . . . "

As he flung her arm away from him his face changed. It had been alight with fury but now it hardened and his mouth thinned into a bitter line. His anger was no longer a blazing inferno but an iceberg, cold and immeasurably deep.

He swung away towards the french door, flinging back the curtain. "I have to return the horse. Tell my uncle I'll be fifteen minutes. Don't delay lunch for me."

6

EVERY nerve in her being was trembling as she watched Eden stride away and swing lithely up to the saddle of the chestnut horse which waited. Until that moment she had thought he was steel all through. It had never occurred to her that he might be hurt by a few careless words.

Abruptly, she turned away. No, she must not feel sorry for him. She would remember his harshness, the hand cruelly tight around her arm, her own fingers closed over the still-throbbing wrist.

Sir Matthew said there was no hurry for lunch as it was to be a cold meal. He went on with the story he was reading to Michael, while Holly stared unseeingly from the sitting room window.

She was still standing there, her arms

folded tightly in an agony of tension, when the black Jaguar roared through the gap and swung round at such speed that grass flew up from the wheels.

"'And so naughty Pickle kitten went to bed without his supper'," Sir Matthew concluded as the main door slammed shut and Eden's boot-heels sounded sharply across the hall.

"You've come just right, Eden," Sir Matthew said cheerfully.

To Holly's amazement, her son slid down from the old man's knee and ran towards the doorway laughing. "Uncle Maffew read a story!"

For a moment Eden stared grimly down at the child, then his expression wavered and he bent to lift Michael into his arms. "Did he indeed? Was it a good story?"

"The kitten had a funny hat on." Michael giggled.

A slow smile warmed Eden's face, as though he could not resist the boy's merriment. "I've a funny hat, too. A cowboy hat. I'll show it to you after lunch. Let's go and wash our hands, shall we?"

Without waiting for Holly's permission, he strode away with the child perched on one strong arm. There seemed to be a big rock in Holly's throat, a ball of tears which threatened to come unstrung and betray her. To see Michael with the old man was bad enough but to watch him with Eden was almost beyond bearing.

"Young Michael is working miracles. Did you see?" Sir Matthew said. "That's the first time I've seen Eden smile since he came home. But nobody could resist your son."

A sense of unreality cushioned Holly as they ate the cold beef salad and the custard tart. Across the table Eden was engrossed in his own thoughts, answering when his uncle spoke to him, but he twice made remarks to Michael and the child responded eagerly, chattering to his new-found friend as if he had known him for all of his short life.

"What time will these people be arriving, Eden?" Sir Matthew asked as Grimson poured coffee.

"I've no idea," Eden replied. "I don't expect them before mid-afternoon."

"And what, exactly, is their reason for coming?"

Eden's mouth tightened and one hand toyed with his coffee spoon. "I'm giving them a scoop, Uncle Matthew. An exclusive." He paused to give more weight to the announcement. "My retirement from the art world."

There was a stunned silence as Sir Matthew stared open-mouthed at his nephew, and Eden sent an unreadable glance at Holly.

"I told Mrs Hastings this morning. She didn't take me seriously."

"I should just think she did not!" Sir Matthew exclaimed. "Eden . . . all you have ever wanted to do is paint, since you were a boy. What has made you come to this decision?"

"Life," Eden said flatly, and again glanced at Holly, making her feel that she was an intruder on this private conversation.

She hastily finished her coffee and asked to be excused, leaving her chair to take Michael's hand.

"I'm going to see the cowboy hat!" Michael protested, trying to squirm free.

"So you are," Eden responded, leaping to his feet. "Come along with me, Michael."

The child pulled his hand free from Holly's grasp and ran to place it trustingly in Eden's, his face lifted with sparkling eyes. Together, the two left the room. Father and son, Holly thought, furious with herself for some reason she did not understand.

Pushing his chair back, Sir Matthew laboriously came to his feet. "Well! What do you make of that, Holly? What on earth did he mean about retiring? Did he explain to you?"

"He only said his muse had deserted him," Holly replied. "And then he said there was no such thing as a muse."

111

She was remembering what had followed, how she had gone to uncover the canvas on the easel and Eden had forcibly restrained her. What was it that he was keeping so secret?

Suddenly Holly caught sight of the time on her watch. Explaining that her son needed his afternoon nap, she headed for the studio but hesitated nervously at the door. What sort of mood would Eden be in now?

"Who's that?" his irritated voice answered her tentative knock.

"It's Holly," she replied. "Is Michael still with you?"

"Come and see," he invited.

She opened the door slowly, and saw Michael sitting on the dais, wearing an enormous stetson hat and a wide, delighted grin.

"It's time for your rest," she said, and winced as Eden loomed up beside her to close the door. In his hand he held a sketch pad and even in one brief glance Holly saw that he had been drawing Michael.

"Don't interrupt," he ordered. "Take a seat and be quiet."

"But Michael needs a nap," she said firmly. "He always does at this time of day."

Eden turned to the child with a gesture of his dark head. "Are you tired, Michael?"

"No," Michael said at once.

"I thought not. Stop fussing, Holly. He's not a baby. He'll sleep much better tonight."

"Which shows how much you know about it?" Holly retorted. "If he doesn't lie down for half an hour he's crabby at tea-time and bad-tempered when I want to bath him. It always happens."

"Well, if it happens today," Eden said levelly, "I'll deal with him myself. How's that for a bargain? Don't stop us now, we've just got into the mood."

He returned to his seat on the floor, the sketch pad on one knee. A glance at Michael and the pencil began to move across the paper, sure strokes bringing the child's figure to life on the page.

Holly remained standing, hands on hips, determined not to be manipulated in this way. But the situation was too piquant for her to retain her annoyance. Eden was sketching his son, if only he knew it.

Unconsciously, her eyes roamed over the deeply-concentrating man. Her hands itched with the desire to run them over that broad back and press her face against curling dark hair which would smell of fresh air and sunlight. A weakening wave of tenderness made her knees feel like jelly and she sat down on the arm of a chair.

She could imagine the lonely boy Eden must have been after he lost his parents. And now something else was hurting him, making him vulnerable to self-doubt and torment. Watching him, Holly had an insane impulse to blurt out that Michael was his son, as if that fact might heal whatever wounds were festering inside him. Ridiculous. If Eden knew the truth he would only be more angry.

Across his shoulder, she could see the sketch developing, detail being added. Michael was beginning to fidget, having sat still for at least five minutes.

"Okay, Michael," Eden said easily. "Come and see."

He held the pad at arm's length and the child scampered across to look at it, one hand on Eden's shoulder.

"It's me!" he squealed.

"Of course it's you." Eden laughed, turning to Holly. "What do you think?"

For the first time he was looking at her without any dark emotions, with a smile that had only pleasure in it, and Holly felt her heart contract painfully.

Smiling, he bore a resemblance to the child in the sketch. If he sat and stared at Michael for much longer he was bound to see the similarity — in eyes, mouth, hair — to the face he shaved every morning.

Her eyes were full of fear, which killed Eden's smile.

"Well?" he said impatiently. "Do you like it?"

"It's marvellous." Her voice was tremulous and his brown creased warningly. "Really!" Holly cried. "Oh, Eden you can't give it up! It'd be crazy. If you really meant it, you wouldn't have wanted to draw Michael."

He slowly came to his knees, then stood up, glowering down at her. "I did it for my own pleasure. That's what it should be. Not wanting acclaim. Not to be lionised at boring parties. Not for wealth, or for women. Just to enjoy creating something beautiful with my own hands."

Her mouth trembled as she stared at him. It was commercialism that Eden was discarding, not his talent itself.

"If you feel like that," she said softly, "you won't stop painting."

"Won't I?" His voice had gone very quiet and menacing, his eyes narrowed to icy slits. His hand came out and fastened in the silky waterfall of her hair, compelling her to her feet in front of him. "No, not yet, perhaps. I have a couple more portraits I want to do.

Your son, for one. And you — you with your innocent angel's face and . . . "

He left the rest unspoken, but this expression made it clear that he was not complimenting her. But how could she blame him — She had herself practically confessed, only that morning, to being a scheming wanton.

Suddenly a tiny whirlwind attacked Eden's legs, crying, "Leave my Mummy alone! Leave my Mummy alone!"

Eden's look of surprise might have been comical at any other time. He instantly released Holly's hair and bent to sweep the yelling child high in the air before swinging him into his arms. Michael went on fighting until a large brown hand captured both of his small ones.

"Michael!" Eden said with forced amusement. "It's all right. Mummy and I were only playing. Only playing."

The child stopped struggling, but frowned into the smiling face with the worried black eyes. Even Holly could see that Eden had forgotten the child's presence in the heat of his anger and was now sorry for the impression he had created in Michael's young mind. He glanced at her anxiously, silently begging for help.

"You tell him, Holly. We were just playing, weren't we?"

"Of course." Her lips felt stiff as she made herself smile, reaching to touch her son's cheek, and at the same moment Eden's arm came round her shoulders.

"Mummy and I are friends, really," Eden told the child, whose questioning gaze flicked from face to face. "You see? We're all friends?"

If only it were true! Holly thought longingly, allowing herself to imagine for one tiny moment that she and Michael and Eden were a family unit, warmly united as they must appear to be at that moment.

It was Michael who broke up the tableau, struggling to be free to play again. Released from Eden's grasp,

Holly stepped back, troubled, watching her son run across the room to where his train was lying on its side.

"You ought to be on the stage," Eden said derisively, and when she looked at him she saw that the moment of togetherness had, indeed, been an illusion, for there was not an ounce of tenderness in his expression.

Tired of bandying words with him, Holly turned to the door.

"Oh, and by the way," Eden added as she was about to leave, "tonight we do dress for dinner. The magazine people will be disappointed if we don't live up to their image of us. Wear that floaty white dress, why don't you?"

In a torment of alternating despair and fury, Holly took herself for a walk on the moor.

She trudged on until she reached the cairn and sat down beside it, her face lifted to the sunlight. She had made a terrible mistake in coming back to Felswithen, as every hour that passed confirmed. But one decision had been made for her — she could never marry Peter. She was too fond of him to offer the little she had to give. For it was only a little, only fondness and gratitude, because the rest belonged to Eden. Hopeless though it was, she had to face the fact.

Absorbed in miserable thoughts, it was some time before she realised that the sky was clouding over. One glance at its broiling turmoil was enough to send her hurrying back towards the dale.

As she reached the edge of the hollow, the shadow of the cloud overtook her and the light turned sickly. Fat drops of rain began to spit down as she edged, crabwise, down the slope, and before she reached the bottom the sky opened and drenched her.

Dripping, gasping, she fled across the hollow and saw a strange grey car outside the house. Grimson was just ushering the visitors into the house. Holly found herself in the hall with a tall, platinum-blonde girl wearing sunglasses, and a weedy-looking man strung about with cameras.

"If you'll wait in the sitting room . . . " Grimson was saying.

"Excuse me," said Holly, making for the stairs, but she stopped as a commotion sounded along the upper hall and Eden appeared at the top of the stairs, doing his best imitation of a galloping horse. Michael was astride his shoulders, dressed in pyjamas and squealing with delight.

"Well, well," the blonde girl said under her breath, pushing her sunglasses to the top of her head. "Eden! Darling, what are you doing?"

He had stopped dead at the top of the stairs, the gloom from the storm making his face indistinct. "Paddy?" he said in disbelief.

"Surprise, surprise!" the girl carolled archly. "You didn't know that little me was working for 'Galaxy,' did you? But I repeat, darling, whatever are you up to?"

"Baby-sitting." Holding Michael's

hands in front of him, Eden came slowly down the stairs.

The girl's high-pitched giggle grated on Holly. "It looks more as though the baby is sitting on you! Who on earth does he belong to?"

"Mrs Hastings here." He had reached the last few steps, his eyes briefly flipping to Holly and away only to flash back again as he saw the wet state she was in. "Good God, what have you been doing?" he exclaimed furiously. "Get upstairs and have a bath before you catch your death!"

"I will," she said tightly. "May I relieve you of my son?"

"He hasn't had his tea yet. Anyway, it looks as though you can't even take care of yourself, let alone a child. For goodness' sake go and get dry."

Angry at being spoken to in that tone in front of strangers, Holly fled up the stairs, tears of mortification adding to the moisture on her face. How she hated Eden Pemberley!

7

THE bathroom, Holly discovered, was almost awash from the splashes on the tiles and the floor. She grabbed a towel to dry her hair, intending to relieve her hosts of the responsibility of Michael, but before she had finished Mrs Grimson brought her a tray of tea.

"I'll be down in a few minutes to take Michael out of their way," Holly said apologetically.

"Who says he's in their way?" the housekeeper demanded. "If you ask me, they're all having a whale of a time. I'll give Michael his tea. He's a bit fractious. Didn't have his afternoon nap, did he? That's why I suggested to Mr Eden that he should have his bath before tea."

"You mean . . . Eden bathed Michael?"

"He said he had promised you he

would. I should have a hot bath, if I were you. Would you like to borrow my hair-dryer?"

Holly gratefully accepted the offer. Beyond the window the rain lashed down from a leaden sky and occasionally distant thunder rumbled in waves of sound across the moor, making Holly shiver.

It was not long before Mrs Grimson brought Michael upstairs and Holly put him to bed. As she had predicted, he was in a bad temper because he was tired, but despite the thunder he was soon asleep once he was tucked in bed with his faithful teddy.

So the reporter had turned out to be a woman, Holly mused as she lay soaking in the bath. For some reason she already disliked the newcomer. Where had Eden met her before?

That is none of your concern, she told herself sharply. What she had to do was decide what to wear. The 'floaty white' had been Eden's suggestion. Perversely, Holly decided she would not allow him to dictate to her. She would wear the deep apricot dress.

Clad in her long bathrobe, she dried her hair with Mrs Grimson's dryer until it ran through her fingers like warm silk. She made up her face carefully before swirling her hair into a knot on the crown of her head, leaving a few feathery tendrils round her face. Then with a nervously-beating heart she stepped into the silk-jersey evening dress. The material clung to her figure, leaving a deep V at the front as she tied the straps into a floppy bow which fell between her shoulder blades. It was the most expensive — and the most revealing — dress she had ever worn.

By that time the thunder was closer, battering the air, and lightning glared beyond the window every few minutes. Another growl of thunder rolled endlessly, and in the middle of the noise a soft tapping came on her door.

"Are you decent?" Eden's voice asked.

Holly's stomach turned over. A glance in the mirror told her that her decency was debatable, but she said, "Yes," and unconsciously lifted her chin, prepared for anything. "Come in."

The door opened and Eden stood there, dressed in tailored black slacks and a ruby-coloured silk shirt. He started to say something which died on his lips as his eyes swept over her in open admiration, making Holly feel hot.

"I know you told me to wear the other one . . . " she began defiantly, and stopped when he laughed, closing the door.

"I knew you would have to be contrary," he replied. "I wanted to see you in this dress."

"How nice it must be to know so much!" Holly said acidly, furious that she should be so predictable.

"It's amusing, sometimes. Anyway, the effect is stunning. Take my word for it."

"Compliments?" she challenged.

"Why not? You merit them, especially tonight. But I was afraid you might not possess the wherewithal to gild the lily." Out from his trouser pocket he brought a glitter of gold and green, square-cut emeralds strung on a fine chain of filigree gold. "These belonged to my mother. No, Holly, it's not another insult, so don't get on your high horse. They are on loan, for tonight."

Holding the gleaming jewels on his palm, the emeralds sparking elfin fire in the light, he advanced purposefully towards her. "Let's see how they look."

As if in a dream, Holly stood docile as he took hold of the wrist which was bruised from his fingers, his touch like fire against her skin as he fastened the bracelet, his dark head bent within inches of her face, making her feel as if her insides were about to melt. When he looked at her his eyes were opaque and he was breathing unevenly, as susceptible to her nearness as she was to his.

"Turn round," he ordered gruffly, and Holly obeyed, held in the spell which she was powerless to break.

His breath was warm on her ear as he draped the emerald collar round her neck, his fingers fumbling with the catch. When it was done, he laid his hands on her shoulders and made her face the full-length mirror.

Holly saw his dark face work as she met his eyes through the glass, and suddenly he whirled her round, into his arms, his mouth possessing hers with a passionate cruelty. After a brief moment of immobility, she lifted her fists and beat at him, her body twisting in a frenzy of resistance.

He lifted his head to stare at her with brilliant dark eyes, relaxing his grip, and with a desperate effort she pulled free, tears dripping from eyes that were brighter than the emeralds around her throat.

"For me there has to be more to it," she said through her tears. "There has to be love, Eden!"

Breathing hard, he glared at her. "You wave that word around like a banner. Love! What does it mean?"

"Don't you know?"

"I thought I did — once — but I had it thrown back in my face. Love is pain and anguish, nothing more. I've vowed never to let that weakness possess me again. But have it your own way. You're not the only woman around any more."

He flung the last sentence at her through clenched teeth, then turned for the door and slammed out, leaving Holly trembling.

Realising that there was still dinner to be endured, she washed her face and re-applied her make-up, but nothing would make her keep on the apricot dress after what had happened. Instead she put on the white chiffon with a print of green leaves. It obscured her figure in layers of floating panels.

Sadly, she took off the emerald collar and bracelet, letting their glitter trickle on to the dressing table. Jewels such as those were not for her, not for plain Holly West from a farm in Sussex.

The party was to have gathered for cocktails at seven thirty, but after that dreadful encounter with Eden it was nearly eight before Holly came silently down the stairs, feeling cold and controlled, so bruised and battered emotionally that nothing else could hurt her.

She opened the sitting room and stood there, pale and composed, her head high. Eden was draped against the chimney breast, one hand gesticulating with a crystal glass that sparked rainbows in the light. He had donned a black velvet jacket on top of the ruby shirt, and added a black bow tie. She saw him smile grimly at her and then she ignored him.

Accepting the cocktail which Grimson brought, she moved into the room saying, "Good evening," to Sir Matthew and apologising for her lateness.

"The wait was well worth it, my dear," the old man approved. "You look delightful." Taking her arm, he introduced her to the two guests — Paddy Waters, and Roy Smith, the photographer.

Holly took a seat on the settee, three feet away from where the other girl was draped in a shimmering silver pants suit which fitted like a second skin.

"We've been hearing all about you," Paddy said, violet eyes appraising. "The fallen tree, and so forth. What an ordeal!"

"It was worse for my aunt," Holly said, peering into her glass as if it were a crystal ball.

"I'm sure I'd have been terrified," the blonde girl said in that pert, clever voice which managed to sound totally insincere. "At least you had a handsome rescuer in Eden. For that I might venture into danger myself, eh, darling?"

She sent a sparkling, intimate look at Eden, who replied drily, "I haven't noticed you being particularly wary of thin ice, Paddy."

131

Paddy decided that Roy must take photographs of everyone. "Eden, darling, if you come and sit between me and . . . Mrs Hastings, is it?"

With very bad grace, Eden sat down beside Holly, who immediately rose and retreated behind the photographer in a whirl of chiffon, saying, "You won't want me in the picture."

"Of course we do," Paddy cooed. "It's a nice human touch — the neighbourliness of the Pemberleys to the orphans of the storm. Do come and sit down."

"I would prefer not to," Holly said with cool determination, and the argument was dropped, though Holly was disturbed by the amused glance which Paddy flung at her.

The photographer used three flash bulbs before Grimson announced dinner. With evident relief, Eden and Sir Matthew rose from their seats, the old man coming to offer Holly his arm. His expression told her that he had already had enough of the publicity charade, and his hand comfortingly patted hers where it lay in the crook of his elbow.

Since there were five people at dinner, Sir Matthew took his place at the head of the table, Eden and Paddy on his left, Holly and Roy Smith to his right, the visitors both as far from their host as was possible.

While Grimson served melon balls and white wine, Paddy flung questions about the house at Sir Matthew.

"I suggest you ask Eden," the old man said eventually. "You've come to talk to him, not to me."

Unabashed by his tone, she laid a hand on Eden's velvet sleeve. "Yes, darling, I shall expect your full attention while I'm here. It isn't every day that Eden Pemberley agrees to give an interview. Do tell me — why did you decide to break your own rule?"

There was a moment's absolute silence, during which Eden sent a hooded glance across the table at Holly. "I thought it might be amusing," he replied. "And I have a reputation for unpredictability. I'm just living up to my image."

"My, my, aren't w enigmatic?" Paddy purred, herself slanting a questioning glance at Holly.

Mrs Grimson had excelled herself with a spectacular crown of lamb for the main course, over which Paddy exclaimed so ecstatically that Holly was disgusted.

"You must show me the moors tomorrow, darling," she said to Eden. "Very dramatic. Very Wuthering Heights. You do ride, don't you? We must have a picture of that — just you on a magnificent horse, galloping across the wild land like a modern Heathcliffe. Our lady readers would adore it."

"I may be busy tomorrow," Eden said shortly. "I'm working on something."

"A picture? Then I'll come and watch. We can talk as you work."

"I don't like an audience," Eden said.

For the first time Paddy seemed to realise that he was not responding to her charms. "You're being very difficult," she said sulkily. "You invited me here."

"I invited a reporter," Eden corrected. "But for the privilege of an interview you'll have to fit in with my schedule."

"What exactly are you working on?" Paddy wanted to know.

"I'm doing a portrait of Mrs Hastings' son."

"Really?" The wide, feline eyes rested with interest on Holly. "A commission?"

"My own choice," Eden said flatly.

Lifting her wine glass, Paddy surveyed Holly over its rim. "That should be charming. It's quite a compliment to be immortalised in oils by Eden Pemberley."

"Michael and I are both flattered," Holly said quietly.

Paddy tossed her short cap of silver-blonde hair, her lips stretching in semblance of a smile. "I'm intrigued,

Mrs Hastings. Where do you come from?"

"From Sussex."

"And you're a widow?" Her eyes rested briefly on the thin gold ring Holly was wearing. "What of your family — your parents?"

"Miss Waters!" Sir Matthew broke in sternly. "Mrs Hastings is a guest in my house. Save your questions for Eden."

She blinked rapidly, feigning embarrassment. "I do beg your pardon, Sir Matthew. I shall gladly confine my attention to your nephew — if he will give me direct answers and not fence with me. The public are entitled to know about one of the great contemporary artists."

"Why are they?" Eden demanded.

"Well, darling, they are your bread and butter."

"Rubbish!" Eden snapped, and leaned across the table to refill Holly's wine glass, looking at her with a veiled expression.

"Oh dear." Paddy smiled, chin in hands again. "You're in one of your black moods, I can tell. That's the problem with the artistic temperament, Mrs Hastings. One is constantly in danger of rubbing against sensitive areas. Don't you agree?"

"I really wouldn't know," Holly said, wondering why she had become the target for the girl's malice.

There was a brief pause while Grimson served fresh fruit salad, then Sir Matthew asked, "How long have you know my nephew, Miss Waters?"

"Oh, aeons," she replied airily. "Isn't that so, darling? Actually, Sir Matthew, I was the one who introduced him to poor Lucy."

"It appears to me," the old man said bluntly, "that you didn't do either of them any favours," which made the girl gape at him — the first genuine expression Holly had seen on her face.

After that, even Paddy seemed to run out of questions and bright remarks.

Although the Pemberleys usually took

coffee in the sitting room, on that evening Sir Matthew asked that it be served at the table.

"We must have some pictures of that Roy," Paddy said to her colleague. "After-dinner cigars and coffee." She turned sideways in her chair, one hand supporting her blonde head as she studied Eden's profile. "You are going to smoke a cigar, aren't you, darling? You always used to."

Holly had become fascinated by the expression on Eden's face. He seemed to be holding some fierce emotion in check, though it was growing stronger with every passing second. A muscle in his jaw jumped erratically and he lifted his eyes to glare at Holly with a fury she could almost feel. His whole body jerked suddenly and his shoe caught Holly's shin a painful blow. She gasped aloud, staring at him in disbelief, and saw the fury melt into anguish.

"Holly, my dear," Sir Matthew said anxiously "Are you all right?"

"Oh — yes." She managed a laugh,

having to stop herself from rubbing the screaming pain in her leg. "Yes, I'm perfectly all right, thank you. I . . . caught my ankle on the table leg."

"You'll have to excuse me," Eden said tautly, pushing his chair back, brushing a distracted hand through his hair as she strode from the room.

"I apologise for my nephew," Sir Matthew said shortly. "He has not been himself since he arrived home."

"He certainly seems to be uptight about something," Paddy drawled, her violet eyes on Holly.

Later, Holly went to check on Michael and examined the dark blue weal across her shin. The area around it was swollen. Eden's reasons for inflicting such a summary punishment were a mystery to her, the more so because the instant he had done it he had looked sorry.

Having made sure that Michael was asleep, she was reluctantly making her way back when Eden appeared at the top of the stairs.

"Don't look like that," he begged, pausing several feet from her. "Did I hurt you?"

"Oh, no!" she retorted with unveiled sarcasm. "I always wear cricket pads under evening dresses."

"I swear to you, Holly," he said earnestly, "I didn't meant to do it. It was sweet of you to lie for me, but I swear it was an accident. Paddy . . . " He gave a weary laugh and leaned against the wall. "Paddy was playing footsie with me, all through the meal. I had to do something violent to stop her, so I shifted my feet and . . . "

"Are you trying to tell me you haven't yet learned how to deal with flirtatious females?" Holly demanded. "I'm astonished! I wouldn't have thought you were afraid of women."

"Paddy isn't just a woman," Eden said with a crooked smile. "She's a human refuse disposal — men being the refuse she chews up and spits out."

"Then she would appear to be an

ideal soul-mate for you," Holly said. "Because you do the same to women!"

Eden stared at her, a strange look on his face, somewhere between pain and amusement with a flicker of anger intermingled. "Touche," he said quietly, lifting a hand towards her face.

Holly withdrew sharply. "Don't touch me!"

His arm slowly fell, to thrust the hand in his pocket. "All right, Holly. If you say so. Just tell me one thing, will you?"

"It depends what it is."

"Earlier this evening," Eden said slowly, as though the words were difficult, "you said that for you . . . for you . . . " His face contorted. He slammed the side of his clenched fist into the wall. "Hell! Why do I bother to ask? I know the answer," and he wrenched himself round to go swiftly down the stairs.

Holly heard him fling open the sitting room door and say loudly, "Well! Here we are then. Sorry to have kept you waiting. Mrs Hastings is on her way. Then we'll begin the interview, shall we? The truth, the whole truth, and nothing but the truth!"

8

EDEN'S 'truth' turned out to be a vilification of the art world — critics, dealers, collectors; all came in for scathing comment. He stood before the log lire which had been lit, holding the attention of his listeners by the magnetism of his personality and the mesmerising use he made of a brandy glass to emphasise points, but he was careful to keep to generalities and never mentioned his private life.

And what, Holly wondered, had he been about to ask her before he stopped himself? What was it she had said? What was the mystery of the covered canvas in the studio? What personal problem was haunting Eden?

Questions, questions, and no answers. The brandy she was sipping was making her thoughts muddled.

Finally, Eden ran out of caustic remarks and fell silent, face grim, long legs straddled with the fire burning behind him.

"Well!" Paddy Waters said with a breathy laugh. "Do you really want me to print that? For your own sake, darling, you ought to sleep on it."

"Why should I feel differently in the morning?" Eden demanded.

"Because tonight you're just a teeny bit tipsy. Be thankful I'm your friend. Anyone else would be rushing to the phone with this scoop." She stood up, straightening her silver jacket. "If you'll excuse me, I'll go to bed. Travelling always tires me out. Goodnight, Sir Matthew, Mrs Hastings. I'm looking forward to meeting your darling little boy again in the morning."

The smile she gave Holly was pure malice, but her back was turned to Eden and his uncle.

Her exit made Roy Smith decide that he was tired, too. His goodnights were mumbled incoherently as he sidled out.

As the door closed, Eden strode across the room to pour himself another measure of brandy.

"You should never have invited them to come," Sir Matthew said with a frown. "That girl is all cat."

"I wasn't to know she was on the staff at 'Galaxy', was I?" Eden replied. "More brandy? What about you, Holly? Oh, be a devil for once. The night is young."

"And you," Sir Matthew said darkly, "are in a most peculiar mood, Eden." As his nephew went to replenish their glasses, the old man shook his head at Holly as if to say that Eden was uncontrollable.

"Tell me," he said as Eden returned, "how long have you known that girl?"

"Paddy?" He gave Holly her brandy, not looking at her. "About four years, on and off. Why?"

"I just wondered."

Eden let out a sharp laugh. "Yes, and I can guess what you were wondering, but you're wrong. We've met at parties, in restaurants. I've never even been alone with her." He threw himself down at the other end of the settee from Holly. He lifted his glass to stare through it at the fire. "Here's to . . . the orphans of the storm." Tossing off half the brandy, he held the glass between his knees. "Of course, you know why she really came?"

Sir Matthew looked puzzled. "For an interview?"

"Not just that." Eden shook his dark, unkempt head. "No, she'll be wanting to get my version of Lucy's death."

"Are you going to give it to her?" the old man asked.

"No. And just in case you're wondering, it isn't because the truth would incriminate me," with a sharp glance at Holly. "The fact is, the truth isn't very pretty. In cold print, it might look as though I was slandering someone who is no longer alive to refute the allegations."

"I see," Sir Matthew said.

Eden looked at him with affection.

"You've never asked me about it, have you? I appreciate that. I appreciate your confidence in me. Not everyone trusts me in quite the same way." He did not, this time, look at Holly, but she felt the criticism was directed at her.

"The truth is," Eden went on, "that I wasn't even with Lucy that night."

"Eden . . . " the old man put in worriedly. "You don't have to . . . "

"Yes, Uncle Matthew," came the quiet reply. "I have to, and I want to. I want you and Holly to know the truth . . . My marriage was all wrong, from the very beginning. Once Lucy had persuaded me to move to America she didn't need me any more, except as a trophy. By that time I didn't care any more, either. I had my work, and that was all I needed, though even that began to seem phoney.

"Anyway, we were invited on this cruise. Lucy's current paramour — a pop singer — was along as well, so I hardly saw her. I slept alone and I spent the days bored out of my mind.

And one morning Lucy was missing. Her boy-friend said he had left her alone on deck the previous night. We backtracked, but we couldn't find her. Her body was washed up about a week later. I can only assume that she had too much to drink and fell overboard.

"Of course, the pop singer and I both came in for some hard questioning, though his manager succeeded in keeping his name out of the papers. There was no evidence of violence, however, so eventually they let us both be. No one will ever know exactly what happened, but I didn't kill her and that's the truth."

"Nobody ever said you did!" the old man protested.

Eden slanted a sardonic smile at Holly. "They did, Uncle Matthew. Lots of people have said it, or thought it. But now that I've told you two I don't care what the rest think."

Bemused, Holly wondered why she had been included in the audience. "Perhaps now you'll be able to relax,"

Sir Matthew said. "I knew you had something on your mind. Why didn't you come home sooner?"

"I'm not sure I ought to have come home at all," Eden replied sombrely. "I'm not sure of anything. Until today I had every intention of giving up painting, but, as Holly so wisely said, that's impossible while I still feel as I do about it. Michael has brought back the itch. I'd like to capture that innocent jollity he has. Maybe that's what I'm in need of myself, but innocence once lost is never regained."

Sighing, Sir Matthew struggled to his feet. "If you're going to get philosophical, I'll leave you. But if you take my advice, Eden, you'll get rid of that pair from London before you say something you'll regret. Goodnight, now. Goodnight, Holly, my dear."

Before he had left the room, Holly was on her feet, shaking out the soft folds of her dress. "I ought to go too. Michael is always up early."

Eden looked up at her, a corner of his mouth lifting wrily. "I was beginning to think you'd lost the power of speech. You haven't said a word all evening."

"What was there to say?" she countered, edging away.

"You might have said you believed that I didn't harm Lucy."

"I never did disbelieve it," Holly told him in a low voice. "Goodnight, Eden."

As she made towards the door, his voice stopped her, saying her name, and she turned to see him standing in front of the fire.

"I was wrong about the dress," he said with an abrupt gesture. "That one is more your style. More . . . demure. Was I wrong about you, too?"

Holly stiffened, her head lifted proudly. "Yes, you were."

"Then I apologise," Eden said gravely. "You said . . . you said that for you there has to be love. Isn't that the way you put it?"

"I meant it," Holly said, though her voice shook.

"Then five years ago . . . you loved me?"

Her hands clenched at her sides, grasping handfuls of chiffon. If she told the truth it would have to be the whole truth — about Michael, about the non-existent husband . . .

"I thought I did," she replied harshly. "I was young and inexperienced. I let myself believe in magic, just for a while."

"And soon afterwards you discovered you had been wrong, because Peter Hastings showed you what true love was all about?"

"Yes!" Holly cried. "Yes, he did! Are there any other personal questions you feel entitled to ask?"

Eden turned away, leaning on the chimney breast, dark head bent as he stared at the fire. "Goodnight, Holly," was all he said.

In tears, Holly fled to her room and flung herself down on the bed, to weep

151

with utter despair into the darkness.

Next morning, the previous evening had taken on a horrible unreality for Holly. Yesterday she had thought she could never marry Peter, but she had already wasted five whole years longing for Eden. Was the future to be as bleak as that?

When she went downstairs she found Michael in the hall, his train and two toy cars using the pattern in the rug as a road.

"Mind the car!" he cried as Holly bent to kiss him. "Look out, Mummy, you're in the way!"

Shaking her head ruefully, Holly straightened and came face to face with Eden, that morning wearing shirt and cords in plain black. He looked dark and attractive, dangerously so.

"Disinterested little beast, isn't he?" he said pleasantly. "Michael, don't you say hello to your Mummy any more?"

Michael looked up, just long enough to say, "Hello, Mummy."

"And what about me?" Eden demanded.

Sitting back on his heels, Michael grinned up at the tall figure in black, and shouted loudly, "Hello, Uncle Eden!"

"Michael . . . " Holly said in horror. "You must say 'Mr Pemberley'."

"Why must he?" Eden asked. "You haven't prevented him from saying 'Uncle Matthew'. Anyway, he can't say Pemberley, can you, Michael?"

"Pemley!" said the child, laughing. "Watch out, Uncle Eden, the train's going to run over you."

Eden stepped back and Holly used the moment to retreat into the dining room. There had been no reason for her objection — no reason she could have explained to Eden, that is. The fact was that it hurt her to hear Michael call his own father 'uncle'. Perhaps she should say so — 'He ought to call you Daddy' The thought made her want to burst into hysterical laughter.

In the dining room, the thin photographer was already breakfasting, alone at the shining expanse of table. Holly helped herself to toast and sat down, pouring coffee for herself and Eden.

"What are your plans for today?" Eden asked the photographer, who almost choked on a mouthful of bacon.

"Paddy wants me to get some shots of you at work, if you don't mind."

"As long as you get it over with," Eden said.

"I'll be leaving later this morning," Roy Smith explained. "We did think . . . that is, Paddy suggested . . . some shots of you with the little boy. You did say you were doing a portrait of him."

Holly drew a sharp breath. Pictures of Eden with Michael? No! Someone was bound to see how alike they were.

"What's the matter, Holly?" Eden asked.

"Nothing," she said shortly.

"Are you sure?"

Irritated, Holly said, "My leg's

154

aching." And had the satisfaction of seeing Eden Pemberley flush with guilt. Except that there was no real satisfaction in it. She felt small and mean, ashamed of herself.

When Paddy Waters appeared, several minutes later, she moved straight to the sideboard without a word of greeting. As she turned with a plate in her hand she shot a look of absolute hatred at Eden and sat down, still wordless, across the table from Holly.

"I'd, er, better check my cameras," the photographer said, pushing his chair back. "Oh — I forgot. The butler said Sir Matthew was having breakfast in bed. Rheumatism, or something."

"Thank you," Eden responded without lifting his head and the thin man departed as if he were glad to escape.

Paddy helped herself to coffee and lifted the cup to her lips, her eyes meeting Holly's with an unfriendly expression. "Well, isn't this cosy? I do hope I'm not intruding. You look a little jaded, Mrs Hastings. Didn't you sleep well?"

"Very well, thank you," Holly said coolly. "Did you?"

"Spasmodically," was the flat answer. "It's very quiet here."

Eden looked up, saying drily, "Very Wuthering Heights. You'll love the moors. All the bogs and the mine-shafts, not to mention the sudden mists. If I were you, I'd take a nice long walk, Paddy."

"Thank you, darling," the girl drawled, eyes glinting. "Mrs Hastings, I hope you'll forgive me, but I'm fascinated by you. You're so young and pretty there must be a tragic story somewhere. What happened to your poor husband?"

As Holly hesitated, wondering where that line of questioning might lead, Eden shifted in his chair so that his thigh touched hers, startling her.

"Would you pour me some more coffee, please, Holly?" he asked politely. "And just ignore Paddy's personal questions. She never did know when to keep her mouth shut."

"But, you see, that's what intrigues me!" Paddy exclaimed. "Why does everyone want to stop me from talking to Mrs Hastings? Your uncle last night, and now you. I'm not entirely stupid."

"Only ninety-nine per cent," Eden rejoined, and for a moment there was open enmity between them as they glared at each other.

Holly re-crossed her legs, stopping that disconcerting contact with Eden, and said evenly, "There's no deep mystery about me. My husband died in a car crash."

"And is there another man in your life?"

"Stop it, Paddy!" Eden rasped. "Sharpen your nasty tongue on me, if you must, but leave Holly out of it."

Holly felt as though her head would burst if they didn't stop fighting over her like two dogs with a bone.

"There is someone," she blurted. "Yes, there is someone waiting for me, and when I go back to Sussex

I'm going to marry him. I wish I was there now. I wish I'd never even heard of Felswithen!"

As she rushed from the room she heard Paddy Waters begin to laugh, the sound tearing at her nerves as she scooped Michael up and carried him headlong up the stairs. She could not face another minute at Hawks High.

Ignoring her son's protests, she put him into his denim jacket and grabbed a long cardigan for herself. She was going to Beck Lodge, to persuade Jo to have her there until she could arrange the journey home. It would also keep Michael away from the photographer. With any luck, she could sneak out through the kitchen.

But luck was not with her, for at the head of the stairs she encountered Sir Matthew, who was walking with a stick.

"Damn rheumatics!" he grumbled. "It always plays up when there's rain. Hello, Michael! You look glum, what's wrong, old chap?"

"He doesn't like being dragged away from his toys," Holly said. "I thought we'd go over to Beck Lodge and see how my aunt is getting on."

"Good idea. Give her my regards, won't you?"

Holly had not realised Eden was there until he spoke from the hall below, saying grimly, "It's a lousy idea. You know I wanted to get on with the portrait this morning."

"Yes, but . . ."

"But nothing!" Eden interrupted. "You can't drag Michael all that way on foot. I'll take you over there this afternoon, if you must go. Come on, Michael. Do you want to wear the cowboy hat again?"

"Yes, yes!" cried Michael, and Holly weakly released his hand, watching him thud inelegantly down the remaining stairs and run to Eden, who swept him up into his arms.

"Tell Mr Smith he can come whenever it suits him," Eden said, departing studio-wards.

Containing a sigh of frustration and fury, Holly walked beside the old man until they reached the hall. It was inevitable now that Roy Smith would get his pictures, whether she liked it or not.

"Eden's right, you know," Sir Matthew said. "It's a very long walk to Beck Lodge for a small child."

"Then perhaps I'll go alone," Holly replied.

Voices along the upper hall warned of the approach of Paddy Waters and her colleague. Sir Matthew grimaced. "I'm off to my study. It's too early in the morning to face that girl again. Will you give them Eden's message?"

Smiling wryly, Holly watched as he hobbled away, reaching the passage as the two unwelcome visitors appeared at the top of the stairs.

"Well, hello again, Mrs Hastings," Paddy called. "Recovered? That was some outburst. Eden isn't the only one who's uptight, is he?"

"I had rather a headache," Holly

replied, waiting until they were level with her. "Mr Pemberley says you can go to the studio whenever you wish."

Paddy's violet eyes were suddenly filled with amusement. "Mr Pemberley? We've gone very formal all of a sudden, haven't we? Roy, darling, go and do your worst. You know what I want."

"Sure," he muttered, nodding.

"Oh, just a moment, Mrs Hastings," Paddy called as Holly turned towards the main door. "I want to have a little chat. Just the two of us, darling."

A 'little chat' with this feline female was the last thing Holly wanted. "I can't stop. I'm going to see my aunt. Excuse me."

"You are nervous," the girl murmured, following her.

Holly stepped out onto the verandah, looking round to say crisply, "Why should I be nervous? I'm just in a hurry."

"Anxious to see your aunt?"

"That's right. Look, Miss Waters,

you came here to interview Eden. Why don't you go and do it?"

"Because he keeps evading my questions. And I'm far more interested in what you can tell me. I'll walk a little way with you, shall I? Keep you company?"

Glancing sceptically down at the girl's high-heeled sandals, Holly said, "You won't get far in those. This isn't Regent Street. Please excuse me." She moved determinedly away, heading straight for the gap in the cliffs.

"Is she really your aunt?" Paddy asked from close behind her.

"Of course she is!"

"Do you expect me to believe that?" came the reply.

Holly swung round, irritated. "It doesn't bother me whether you believe it or not. It happens to be true."

"Very well." Bright eyes swung up and down Holly's figure. "I'll believe you. And since we're being honest with each other, will you tell me something else? Did Eden know you would be here when he arrived home from the States?"

"Eden?" Holly was puzzled. "No, how could he? I only came to Yorkshire that same day. No one could have anticipated the tree coming down."

"Ah, I see. You mean, he knew you would be at your aunt's, but he didn't expect you at Hawks High?"

"I mean he didn't know I would be anywhere within a hundred miles of here!" Holly explained. "What has that to do with anything?"

"Oh, everything," Paddy answered enigmatically. "I mean, if he had known you were here, he would hardly have invited journalists, too, now would he?"

Holly had lost contact with the meaning of this conversation. Paddy seemed to be trying to engage her in some kind of guessing game. "Why wouldn't he?" she asked.

"So innocent!" Paddy laughed. "You do that very well, you know. You've almost faltered a couple of times, but the rest you've carried off beautifully. Eden, too. He's obviously a born actor."

"I'm afraid," Holly said with a bewildered shake of the head, "that I haven't the least idea what you're talking about."

Suddenly Paddy threw back her head and laughed aloud. "You must really think I'm blind! I knew it the moment I saw them, so alike that there couldn't be any doubt. Why, Michael even has his father's temper. He's Eden's son, isn't he?"

9

HOLLY felt that she was drowning, choking with horror and fear. She had thought she was safe, that no one but herself would notice how like Eden the child was, and now this awful girl . . .

"Yes, I thought so," Paddy said, interpreting Holly's expression correctly. "So it must have been going on for a long time, even before Eden met Lucy. Why did he marry her? Couldn't you get a divorce?"

"You're wrong!" Holly croaked, held transfixed by alarm.

"Oh, no, I'm not. It all fits. What were you doing — paying a surprise visit? I'm surprised Eden didn't cancel the interview. Is your husband really dead?"

A shudder ran through Holly and she was at last able to breathe again. "Have you ever said anything about this to Eden?"

"Not yet. But I intend to. He can tell me the rest himself." She began to turn away, but Holly put out a shaking hand and grasped her arm, begging her, "Please . . . don't! Don't tell Eden."

"Why not? You'll tell him yourself, won't you?"

Holly shook her head, lips pressed together in agony. "I can't! You see, he . . . he doesn't know."

"Doesn't know?" Paddy repeated. "Doesn't know what?"

"That . . . " With a heavy sigh of defeat, Holly decided to be honest. It was her only chance of preventing a terrible scene with Eden. "He doesn't know that Michael is his son. Five years ago, I was staying with my aunt. Eden painted my portrait, and . . . I fell in love with him. After I left he didn't try to contact me, so when I found I was pregnant I didn't let him know."

"And nobody realised . . . "

"I've had to lie in my teeth," Holly

166

confessed. "But I'm the only one who knows the identity of Michael's father. At least, I was, until now."

She stopped awkwardly as Paddy's clear laughter floated across the hollow.

"Please don't say anything to him," Holly pleaded.

The violet eyes were brimming with spiteful glee. "Why not? I'd love to see his face. What will he do, I wonder? What will he do?"

The girl was enjoying herself. Holly had no idea what she would do, but she had done all the begging she intended to do. Turning away, she began to run through the clef where the tall rocks threw shadows across the road.

Twenty minutes later, Holly climbed slowly up the stiff climb towards Beck Lodge. The great tree now lay across the yard, denuded of its branches, and two workmen with an electric saw were cutting the trunk into logs. They ceased their activity as Holly came round the corner of the house, one of them

167

cuffing sweat from his forehead and grinning at her.

"Hello, beautiful."

"Good morning," Holly replied, too distraught to respond to the friendliness in his manner. "Is Mrs Dailie in?"

"'Fraid not. She went into the village not ten minutes ago since."

Frowning, Holly surveyed the silent house. "Did she say how long she would be?"

"Not long. But the door's open. If you're going to wait for her, how about making us a cup of coffee? This is thirsty work."

Having taken the workmen their drinks, Holly wandered through the house and up the stairs. In the back bedroom all the furniture had been removed. The protective sheeting which had been put across the hole was torn and the floor beneath it very wet. Probably the storm had beaten in. The bedroom was unusable.

There remained the smaller room at the front, but to Holly's dismay it was full of furniture from the damaged room. Not even one person could sleep in there, let alone two. Despair wrenched through Holly and she leaned on a chest weeping inconsolably. She had so desperately hoped that she and Michael might return to Beck Lodge that very day.

Some indefinable time later, she heard a car approaching from the direction of Hawks High. Eden! She thought with a stab of fear, but the car which nosed up from the dip was not Eden's Jaguar: it was the grey saloon in which Paddy Walters and Roy Smith had arrived. Of course, the photographer had said he was leaving that morning. When would Paddy leave? Would she, before that time, tell Eden that Michael was his son?

Tearing herself away from the rising tide of hysteria, Holly ran back down the stairs and stood staring at the copy of the portrait which had started the whole mess.

With relief, she heard the unmistakable

sound of the land-rover's engine, becoming a roar as it took the last slope and swung round to park. Holly hurried to the window, only to draw back in alarm as she saw Eden's car purr almost soundlessly into place beside the land-rover.

Her aunt, removing parcels from the back of the vehicle, chatted and smiled to the black-clad Eden and the bright-faced Michael, and Eden seemed relaxed enough as he relieved Jo of her burdens.

"What a lovely surprise!" Jo greeted as she kissed Holly's cheek. "I'm sorry I was out."

Taking Michael's hand tightly, Holly followed her aunt into the kitchen, watching as Eden set the shopping on the table. A pulse in her throat throbbed nervously, because he might be keeping his temper for her aunt's sake.

Jo sat Michael at the table and gave him a biscuit before setting about making coffee. Behind her back,

Eden caught Holly's eye, his own gaze narrowing.

"Have you been crying?"

"No!" Holly lied.

"Well, what was the rush? I did say I would bring you."

"You also said you would be busy."

"I was, until Michael had had enough." He rubbed the child's hair with a roughly affectionate hand. "So we thought we'd have a ride and fetch Mummy home, didn't we, Michael?"

Across the kitchen, Jo gave Holly a sharp, questioning look which stabbed through her like a sword.

"What about Paddy?" she asked anxiously. She had to know.

"Paddy decided to cut her losses," Eden said tersely. "She left with Mr Smith."

"She did?" She could hardly believe that Paddy had gone — gone, it seemed, without revealing Holly's secret.

"Have you had a look upstairs?" Jo asked. "It's a mess. I was mopping up half the night, and then the builder didn't turn up. I was hoping to be able to accommodate you by tomorrow, but . . . "

"Don't worry about it," Eden broke in. "They're both welcome to stay at Hawks High for as long as they wish."

"I can't!" The words were torn out of Holly. "Well, I really can't impose any longer. It's not fair to any of you. If we catch the early train tomorrow, we can go back the way we came and be in Sussex before dark."

"But you've only been here for three days," Eden objected. "It was supposed to be a real holiday. Surely he'll wait a bit longer?"

Startled, Holly shot a worried glance at him, but his expression was unreadable.

"He?" Jo said sharply.

"I . . . I told them about . . . about . . . " Holly faltered.

"About Peter?" said Jo, sounding pleased. "Oh, I'm glad. Have you decided to accept his proposal?"

A little frown appeared between

Eden's dark brows as he watched Holly's face. "Peter?" he said quietly.

Holly felt like a trapped bird fluttering in a cage. She had told Eden that her 'husband's' name was Peter. "It's a coincidence, that's all," she said. "We ought to be going. Lunch will be ready."

"I'll just finish my coffee," Eden said, but his look added that he was not content to leave it at that.

Holly's mind was in a panic as she took Michael out to the car, but she reminded herself that she need only keep up the charade for one more day. If she kept cool, it might still be possible to keep anyone from discovering her secret.

The car slid down the slope to the road turning left on to the drop into the dale, its engine sounding sweet between the dry-stone walls.

"Just tell me one thing," Eden said grimly. "Just a simple yes or no, and for God's sake give me the truth this time! Is there a man called Peter who is waiting for you to go back and marry him?"

His face was a mask, strong hands clasped tightly on the wheel.

Holly took a deep breath. "Yes."

"Then why didn't you say so before?"

"You didn't ask," she replied in a small voice.

Eden swore succinctly under his breath, his face like thunder as he swung the Jaguar along the winding road, up to the gap.

"Do something for me," he said as they parked the car. "Don't take Michael away until I've finished the portrait. I know I have no right to ask you for any favours after the way I've behaved, but do that small thing for me. Just a few days more. Please! It's important to me, Holly."

She looked down at Michael, standing between them with upturned face a chubby replica of Eden's. "Very well," she said with a sigh of defeat. "A few more days."

During the afternoon, Eden and Michael retired to the studio for half an hour before the child had his rest. Eden, it seemed, had learned that a four-year-old did need a short nap in the afternoon. Deciding to stay out of the way, Holly stayed chatting to Sir Matthew, who predicted more rain before long. His aching leg told him so.

After precisely half an hour, Eden brought Michael to the sitting room. Michael was not too pleased to be taken to bed, but Holly gave him his teddy and a book to look at, knowing he would soon settle down. It occurred to her that very shortly he would no long need the extra rest. Only one year from now he would be starting school.

And by that time she would be, in truth, Mrs Peter Hastings. The realisation made her want to weep, for reasons which she understood only too well.

She decided to wait in her room until

Michael woke, but had not been there very long when Grimson came with a message to say that Eden wanted to see her urgently in the studio.

Wondering what the summons meant, Holly walked with uneasy steps down the long passage. The studio door stood open and Eden was pacing the room with long, jerky strides, passing by the smaller easel which supported a picture of Michael roughly sketched in against a blue background. He stopped dead when he saw her, giving her such a ferocious look that her heart turned over in fear.

"Come in," he snapped. "Oh, don't worry, I'll keep my distance, if it's humanly possible. I'd better. If I come too near I might easily decide to throttle you. Close the door!"

"Don't speak to me in that tone!" Holly returned, her own temper sparking. "If you can't be civil . . . " She moved hurriedly away as he took two huge strides and closed the door. "What have I done now?" she demanded.

"Done?" he repeated menacingly. "Don't you know what you've done? I had a phone call a few minutes ago. From Paddy Waters. It seems that you and she had a little heart-to-heart before she left."

Shock doused Holly in ice. Her face grew so pale that even her lips were white. She tried to speak, but no words would come.

"My God!" Eden said under his breath. "It is true! He's my child, isn't he? Michael is my son."

"He's not!" she cried. "He's mine. I've never asked you for anything, have I? If it hadn't been for that spiteful . . . "

"Be quiet!" Eden cut her off, his voice like a whiplash across her nerves. "Just tell me — when was he born?"

Holly could no longer control her shaking limbs. She was shivering as if with argue, confronting a scene from her worst nightmare. "M-May the twenty-first, four years ago."

"Then why did you say he wasn't

yet four?" Eden demanded.

"Because you could have worked it out. I didn't want you to . . . "

"Damn you, Holly!" he raged. "My own child. You took my son and gave him another man's name. And now you plan to do it again! Who is this second Peter? What does he do for a living?"

"He — he manages a supermarket."

"A supermarket?" He took a step towards her, his face demoniacal. "How can he possibly give Michael more than I can?"

"He can't, not the way you mean. But he promised to love Michael as if he was his own."

Eden let out a sound that was almost a howl of pain. "His own! But he's not. He's mine!"

"Th-that doesn't matter. We'll never apply to you for help. I haven't done it so far. He won't be a burden."

"A burden?" He stared at her as if she were mad. "A burden? My own son? Good God, why didn't you tell me? Didn't you know I would have . . . "

"Would have what?" Holly asked in agitation. "Sent me money, and hated me for it? Married me, and hated me for that? Hated Michael, too, for spoiling your life? I always knew you never regarded me as anything but a summer toy. I was just another amusement, wasn't I? You do like to be amused, don't you?"

"That's enough!" Eden rasped, taking another long stride, poised as if he would like to launch himself on her. "Thank you for your assessment of my character. But let me tell you something, Mrs Hastings. No other man is going to have the pleasure of bringing up my son for me. I intend to do that."

"Suppose I don't let you?" Holly cried.

His smile was horrible to see, his voice turning silky. "Let me? Oh, my dear Mrs Hastings, you are not understanding me. I'm not asking for

179

permission, I'm telling you how it will be. By all means go and marry your shop-keeper. I shan't attempt to dissuade you." His face was craggy with cruelty as he flung the last sentence. "But my son stays here with me!"

Holly was frozen, shaking from head to foot, disbelieving her ears because this was even more awful than she had dreaded.

"You can't!" she choked.

"Can't I? Try me, Holly. I'll drag you through every court in the land, if I have to. Can you afford a law suit?"

"W-would you deprive him of his mother's love?"

"Why not?" Eden shouted. "You deprived him of mine!"

"You need never have known!" she yelled, in tears now. "Oh, you can't do it. Eden. You can't take him away from me!"

Eden folded muscular arms across his chest, looking at her from under lowered brows, and his voice was cold.

"How would you fancy a job as his nanny?"

Sobbing, Holly broke and ran for the french door, not knowing where she was going. She just had to get away from the pain of what he was threatening. She was hardly aware of scrambling up the hillside, coming to the moor. She ran on, fleeing from something which came right behind her, which would catch her if she paused.

At last her steps faltered, her strength completely gone, and she threw herself down on the springy hummocks, sobbing until her body ached.

She never knew whether she fell asleep or whether the grief overwhelmed her other senses so entirely that she was incapable of noticing the tenuous drifts of mist which began to float across the moor. When she did become aware of them she sat up, numbly puzzled. The mist was like ethereal candy-floss, dissolving beneath the touch, breathing coldly on her face as it passed, floating

181

on across the moor, white against the blue of the sky and the dark mulberry of the heather.

Suddenly realising what it meant, Holly whirled — and faced a wall of that whiteness coming inexorably towards her, blotting out the sun. It was not mist, it was clouds, low clouds such as had crowned the hills on the day she arrived.

10

TORN by conflicting emotions, Eden eventually sought out his uncle, who was in his study warming his aching leg by a fire which made the room seem stifling.

"Come in, my boy," the old man said, noting the tension on his nephew's face as Eden sat in the chair by the desk.

"There's something I have to tell you," he said abruptly, leaning on his knees with his strong hands clenched between them. "I . . . I knew Holly rather better than I led you to believe. You remember 'Girl in the Heather'?"

"Of course. It was Holly, was it not?"

Eden's dark head came up with a jerk. "How did you know?"

"I knew the moment I saw her, though I had no idea, until she walked in here, that the girl in the portrait was Mrs Dailie's niece. You loved her, did you not? Why do you think I've been so anxious for her to stay?"

"Match-making?" Eden's smile was bitter. "Thank you, but it hasn't worked. She hates me even more now than when she arrived. And the worst of it is, Uncle Matthew — Michael is my child."

"Eden!" Sir Matthew sat up in his chair, staring incredulously.

"It's true, I'm afraid," Eden said sorrowfully. "Now that you know, can't you see the likeness? As soon as she told me . . ."

"Holly told you?"

"No, not Holly! Holly would have kept it from me if it killed her. But Paddy guessed. She already suspected — wrongly — that Holly was my mistress, so the equation was easy for her. She taunted Holly into confessing. So dear Paddy phoned me."

Sir Matthew considered the implications of that, one hand massaging his leg.

"Have you spoken to Holly about it?"

With a weary laugh, Eden stood up and turned to stare unseeingly out of the window. "Spoken to her, yelled at her, threatened her — all the wrong things. I was so angry I even said I would take Michael away from her. I stood there saying all the worst things I could think of, until she looked as if she had been whipped." He swung round, hands out in appeal. "Uncle Matthew, how am I ever going to apologise?"

"You must go to her," the old man said at once. "Swallow your stubborn pride, Eden, and tell her the truth."

"If she'll listen," Eden said dully. "I've lost her now. And Michael, too. She's going home to marry some shop-keeper."

"Well, instead of feeling sorry for yourself, go and talk to her," the old man advised.

"I will, as soon as she comes back. She's gone . . . " He stopped, appalled, seeing that beyond the window there was a light drizzle falling from the heavy layer of cloud which draped its tendrils of mist across the hollow.

"Oh, my God!" he got out in a strangled voice. "She's out on the moor!"

★ ★ ★

When she first heard the call she thought it was an illusion. She lifted her head, seeing nothing but mist and heather.

"Holly!" the voice came faintly. It sounded like Eden. Thank God.

"Eden!" she called, though it was thin, swallowed by the mist. Gathering her forces, she shouted again, "Eden!" She unlocked her arms from around her knees and painfully forced herself upright.

The mist parted for a moment, letting her see his tall figure some distance away. She called again and just before the cloud blotted him from sight he saw her.

"Eden!" She cared about nothing but that he should come. No quarrels mattered, only his presence, real and solid. Through chattering teeth she called his name again.

Suddenly he was there, appearing through wraiths of mist. Holly tried to move but her legs wouldn't hold her and she fell into his arms, clinging tightly to him.

"Wait!" Eden said, untangling her arms from his neck. He opened the heavy sheepskin jacket he was wearing and let her inside, against his blessed warmth. Drawing the coat across her back he held it there, held her closely with his cheek pressed against her hair.

"I was so frightened," Holly whispered, shuddering.

"So was I." His voice was hoarse, his arms like steel bands for a moment before he took off the jacket and wrapped it round her; then he lifted her into his arms and carried her through the mist.

"Eden." she said quietly. "Please don't take Michael away from me."

"No."

Astonished, Holly drew back her head so that she could see his face. "You won't? But you said . . . "

"I know what I said. And I'm sorry. I said a great many things I didn't mean. I do that when I'm angry. My tongue runs away with me."

"So does mine," Holly admitted softly.

Sighing, Eden bent to set her on her feet. They were on the edge of the hollow, light rain falling round them and the great grey house waiting below. They slowly made a zig-zag descent, Eden going first, his hand clamped firmly round hers to prevent her from falling. And as they reached the bottom of the slope, a car came slowly through the gap.

The man who climbed out was sandy-haired, wearing a blue anorak. Holly stared at him in disbelief. What was Peter Hastings doing here?

188

"Heavens!" he said with attempted humour. "You do look wet, Holly. This is Hawks High, isn't it?"

Holly was holding Eden's hand very tightly, though she was unaware of it. She was afraid that she might be going to scream, or something equally embarrassing.

"It is," Eden replied tersely. "What can we do for you?"

"Oh, I . . . " Peter seemed nonplussed. "I came to see Holly."

"You'd better come into the house," Eden said, leading the way and taking Holly with him. She was unable to do anything of her own volition.

In the hall they were met by an anxious Sir Matthew, who exclaimed thankfully over Holly's safety and ushered them into the sitting room, where the fire had been lit. Michael was in there, with his train rattling merrily round its track.

"We appear to have a visitor," Eden said to his uncle. "A friend of Holly's. He hasn't given me his name yet."

"Uncle Peter!" Michael cried, on cue, running to take the man's hand. "Come see my train."

Hopelessly, Holly glanced at Eden. His face beneath the dripping wet hair was terrible to see.

"It's Peter," she said stupidly, and suddenly the coat round her shoulders seemed heavy as lead; the room spun around Eden's ravaged face and there was more white mist, claiming her.

As she fell, Eden lunged to catch her. She lolled in his arms, her face ghastly white, her hair spilling across his black shirt. Ignoring Michael's cry of alarm, he turned and strode with Holly into the hall, shouting for Mrs Grimson.

Holly found herself lying on the bed, alone with the housekeeper, who was kind but practical. She made Holly take off her wet clothes and brought her some hot, strong tea before running a bath.

She dressed slowly, in jeans and sweater, not caring how she looked. Why had Peter come? What would he say? Now Holly had to face the two men in her life and tell them she had lied to them both. But whatever came of it, at least she could be at peace with herself.

She was summoning all her courage to face the ordeal when Grimson came to see if she was well enough for another interview with Eden in the studio.

"Yes, I'll come," Holly said, thinking that nothing could be as bad as their last meeting in that huge room. And he had said he would not try to take Michael away from her.

She found Eden sitting morosely on the dais, beside the covered canvas on the big easel. He had changed his wet clothes, too, and now a white sweater showed up his deep tan. But when he looked up she was stricken by the sadness in his eyes.

"You . . . " The word caught in her throat. "You wanted to see me?"

"How are you feeling?" Eden asked.

"Better, thank you. It was just . . . "

"I know what it was," he said quietly. "I blame myself entirely. I'll never be able to apologise sufficiently. Your Peter is in the sitting room with my uncle and Michael. You can see him shortly. I wanted . . . to show you something."

He stood up and with one wide movement threw off the covering sheet from the picture, revealing the original painting he had done five years before. It was even more life-like than the copy — the girl with the dreamy smile and glowing face.

Holly stared at it, bewildered. "But . . . my aunt said it was on exhibition in London."

"It was, for a few months. I had a lot of offers to buy it." His voice had gone husky. "I refused them all. You know why?"

She shook her head, wishing he wouldn't look so wretched.

"Because it was all I had left of you," Eden said.

Pain wrenched through Holly, swiftly

followed by doubt. "But . . . if you felt that way, why didn't you answer my letter?"

"Letter?"

"You must have had it!" Holly exclaimed. "I told you I had to leave suddenly because my grandfather was ill. I left you my address and asked you to write. Eden, you can't have forgotten! I left the letter with Aunt Jo. She promised to give it to you."

Eden was silent for a moment, though his lips formed an unspoken curse. "I never saw it, Holly. When I went to see what had happened to you your aunt told me . . . she said you had decided to leave on the spur of the moment, that you were like that — impulsive. She refused to give me your address. She said that you were little more than a child, flattered by the attentions of an older man, but not to be taken seriously. She sounded very reasonable and wise, and I . . . damn it, I believed her!"

"But . . . " She swallowed thickly. "I

thought you didn't care. That autumn you were all over the gossip columns, with different women . . . "

"Didn't care?" Eden echoed, voice and eyes full of pain. "Good grief, I nearly went crazy! I was doing the social round to try to get you out of my mind. When it didn't work, I fetched this picture out of the gallery and brought it home. I begged your aunt to tell me where you were and she said. she said there was no point because you had already married someone else."

"Oh, Eden!" she managed through her tears. "I didn't betray you. There was no marriage, no husband."

He sighed heavily. "I know. Your Peter told me. He tried to bluff it out but he couldn't keep it up, even though your aunt had primed him well. She has a lot to answer for, Holly. She sent for Peter, you know. She was determined to break us up."

"Only because she thought she was protecting me! Did you . . . did you tell Peter about Michael?"

"No. He still thinks Michael belongs to this student you invented. But he's going to have to know the truth, Holly. I want to provide for my son, I want to have him here for holidays. I hope you'll allow me that much."

She was swaying where she stood, her whole body tensed. "Eden . . . I can't marry Peter. I can't! It would never have worked, because . . . because I love you. I've never stopped loving you."

The joy on his face made her heart leap in response. He took a step towards her, stopped himself. "Even after the way I've behaved these last few days?"

"Oh, Eden! You were hurting. I understand that now. It's been awful for me, too. I was terrified you might find out about Michael, and so afraid you might see how I felt about you . . . "

They met in the centre of the room, his arms enveloping her, his mouth seeking hers with feverish kisses, his body hard and unyielding against hers, making her blood sing.

"I love you," he murmured, his lips buried in the curve of her throat. "Oh, how I love you! Never leave me, Holly."

"Never," she vowed, lifting his head, her hands either side of his brown face. With shining eyes she followed every angle of his face, letting his image imprint itself on her heart.

"There's only one thing," he said. "When this news gets out, I want the world to know that Michael is mine. Will you mind?"

"I don't care who knows now," she replied. "I love you. Oh, why didn't I have the courage to say that before now?"

A smile curved his lips as he tenderly drew her closer. "Better late than never, for both of us. We'll be married as soon as possible. We've already wasted five whole years."

"Oh Eden . . . what about Peter? How am I going to tell him . . . ?"

"I think you'll find that he won't

be too upset," Eden assured her. "I wasn't going to tell you, but he said he asked you to marry him because your grandfather had asked him to take care of you. I shall be only too happy to relieve him of the responsibility."

Holly looked up at him, objecting, "Anybody would think I was incapable of taking care of myself!"

"Well, you are," he said with a laugh. "Anyone who gets soaked on the moors two days running needs someone to keep an eye on her."

"Beast!" She reached up to kiss him and for a while there were no more words. There was only joy, in a world where only the two of them existed.

The real world came back abruptly as something scrabbled at the door handle. Holly and Eden broke apart as Michael came in, frowning, his train in one hand.

"It's broked again!" he complained.

Laughing, Eden swept his son into his arms and drew Holly to him so that the three of them were close together.

"It probably needs a new battery," he told Michael.

The little boy looked at him trustingly. "You fix it, Uncle Eden."

And Eden smiled at Holly. "We shall have to tell him about that," he said peacefully.

THE END

WITH SOMEBODY ELSE
Theresa Charles

Rosamond sets off for Cornwall with Hugo to meet his family, blissfully unaware of the shocks in store for her.

A SUMMER FOR STRANGERS
Claire Hamilton

Because she had lost her job, her flat and she had no money, Tabitha agreed to pose as Adam's future wife although she believed the scheme to be deceitful and cruel.

VILLA OF SINGING WATER
Angela Petron

The disquieting incidents that occurred at the Vatican and the Colosseum did not trouble Jan at first, but then they became increasingly unpleasant and alarming.

DOCTOR NAPIER'S NURSE
Pauline Ash

When cousins Midge and Derry are entered as probationer nurses on the same day but at different hospitals they agree to exchange identities.

A GIRL LIKE JULIE
Louise Ellis

Caroline absolutely adored Hugh Barrington, but then Julie Crane came into their lives. Julie was the kind of girl who attracts men without even trying.

COUNTRY DOCTOR
Paula Lindsay

When Evan Richmond bought a practice in a remote country village he did not realise that a casual encounter would lead to the loss of his heart.

ENCORE
Helga Moray

Craig and Janet realise that their true happiness lies with each other, but it is only under traumatic circumstances that they can be reunited.

NICOLETTE
Ivy Preston

When Grant Alston came back into her life, Nicolette was faced with a dilemma. Should she follow the path of duty or the path of love?

THE GOLDEN PUMA
Margaret Way

Catherine's time was spent looking after her father's Queensland farm. But what life was there without David, who wasn't interested in her?